After trying scaffolding, teaching and bookselling – not to mention trawler-hand, lumberjack and short-order cook in a greasy-spoon – Laurence James spent several years publishing other people's books. In 1973 he decided it was time to try it for himself (writing, that is) and has since had several short stories published both in England and the United States. There has also been a wealth of novels under a proliferation of pseudonyms in a variety of categories. The *Simon Rack* novels have been published with great success on both sides of the Atlantic.

Laurence now lives in a small village in East Hertfordshire with his attractive wife and their three young children. His likes include John Stewart, Buddy Holly, The Drifters and Sha Na Na. His dislikes still include earwigs, suits and gherkins.

D1325300

Simon Rack
New Life For Old
LAURENCE JAMES

SPHERE BOOKS LIMITED
30/32 Gray's Inn Road, London WC1X 8JL

First published in Great Britain by Sphere Books Ltd 1975
Copyright © Laurence James 1975

Set in Intertype Lectura

Printed in Great Britain by
Hazell Watson & Viney Ltd
Aylesbury, Bucks

This is for John Harvey with every good wish as he sets out on the long and winding road. Remember, a sufficient income and then as much art as you know how to produce

ONE

DENY, DEFY OR CRUCIFY YOU

'PARADISE NOW!!'

The letters were in special glowing plasprint, shimmering off the silvery page.

The shuttle motors warmed up, a gust of recycled air fluttering at the brochure, making it hard to read. Ensign Bogart, of the Galactic Security Service, grunted a curse, and eased his neck in the stiff collar of his best dress uniform. The weather on Crucis was warm, up in the thirties, the twin suns gleaming purple in the cloudless sky.

'How much longer, Simon? I'm melting away inside these number ones.'

His companion, taller and younger, was Commander Simon Kennedy Rack, also of GalSec. He smiled at the mutterings of his stocky colleague. Neither of them had much time for the necessities of service protocol, being happier out on a mission in their two-man scout ship. But this was a special one, and they had to put up with it.

'Go on, Bogie. Read out the rest of the ad-card on Paradise. Pass the time.'

'All right, Simon. I tell you, I'll . . .'

'Be glad when this one is over,' finished Simon. 'You say that every time. Get on with it.'

The media men were still busy filming and vidding the departing party, lights flashing and mikes thrusting forward like a hedge of noise. Bogart stretched his shoulders, sighing as one of the shoulder seams proved incapable of taking the strain and opened for a few centimetres like a grey mouth.

'Paradise Now! What a selling line. Right, here goes. If I drown in all these rich adjectives, dive in after me, Simon.'

The brochure was superbly expensive, as befitted something that advertised one of the most costly and unusual trips in the galaxy. It circulated only among the élite of the many worlds that fringed on Crucis. Not the richest five per cent. Or even one per cent. But one half of one per cent *of* one per cent.

And that made it very exclusive indeed.

' "Throughout the ages of man the thought has always been that when you go, you cannot take anything with you. All those credits will pass on to the authorities or to other people, while you enter the realms of those who have gone before.

' "Now you CAN take it with you. In fact, you don't even have to go. Thanks to the most remarkable scientific research ever undertaken by private concerns, CRYOGENICS has now become a reality. But take heed. It is not just that simple. Nor is it that cheap. Details of the costs and of the initial contractual regulations are to be found in the extra sheet at the back of this brochure." '

Bogie grunted. 'Enough small print there to stifle a starship. Packed with those drecky legal phrases that make my blood freeze. "Whereas . . . Notwithstanding . . . Inasmuch as . . . Hereinafter . . . !" That sort of thing. *And* it doesn't mention the price anywhere.'

'Don't want to frighten the game away.'

'At a million credits just for an initial consultation with the offices here on Crucis! There can't be many that don't frighten away. Don't know what it does to that lot, but it terrifies me. And that's for starters.

' "We are not just offering you the chance to save some of your capital. YOUR capital. Nor do we offer some quacksalver remedy to save you ageing. We offer you EVERYTHING!!!!" '

The last word was so designed that it seemed to burn its way off the page and, when exposed to light, the paper with it on

8

was prepared to give off a deep, sonorous chord, filled with the important sound of immortality.

But that was at the end. Bogie was still wading through the rich pastures at the beginning of the booklet, boggling at the pictures, just picking out a phrase here and there to chew over. And spit out.

' "The finest techniques . . . silence if you wish it, and, if you wish it, the finest music in the history of the galaxy . . . Any sensation can be yours, with any kind of stimulus to the sense . . .." ' The roar of the shuttle's engine nearly drowned him out, but he battled on against it. 'I don't see how they can offer that without using dopers.'

'The station's in deep space, Bogie. By the time you tried to bust them for that, they'd have the stuff vaporised. No way they wouldn't see you coming. Anyway, we don't want to bust them. Word is from *very* high up that they're to be left alone. Nobody knows how gen it is, but the men at the top are leaving them to get on with it. It's not doing any harm to anyone. Except denting their credit balance a bit.'

'Listen. "Paradise is nothing and Paradise is everything. Paradise is what you want. No more and certainly no less. As you pass your last seven days in your present time, the staff will cater for your every need. No food we can't prepare. No drink we cannot concoct. No experience that you cannot enjoy as you prepare for your sleep that will lead to the new awakening." Frankly, it makes me want to throw up.'

'Why?' Simon kept glancing round at the crowds, safely penned back behind a layer of local police. There had been the usual crank threats, and there were some important men and women about to join them.

'All right, Simon. For years everyone's thought that science would have come up with immortality. Even back before the darkness. The pre-neutronic scientists talked about curing this and curing that. All they did was blow up Sol Three and nearly wipe man off the face of space.'

This was one of Bogie's favourite hobby-horses coming up. Simon tensed and flexed the muscles at the back of his calves, like his first drill instructor had told him when he joined GalSec thirteen years ago at the minimum age of fourteen.*

'Now everyone knows that cryogenics has been talked about for nearly as long. It's immortality for the rich. We freeze your body before you die, and we can revive you in ten or a hundred or a million years, when they can cure whatever you've got. Even old age! But it never worked. Now this bastard appears from right out of nowhere, and he sells his Paradise. An island in the sky to come to and spend your last week, then off into the capsules for as long as you like. If, what's his name . . .' He fumbled through the booklet for the man he wanted. 'Here . . . "Under the control of Abraham Razan." Look at him. Must be about two metres tall, at least. Who is he and where the hell did he come from to be able to do what nobody ever managed before?'

At last it looked as though the media men were tiring of their exalted quarries, and a few vids were flashing away now at Simon and Bogie. One young girl in a thigh-slit green tunic pushed a mike at Simon. 'Commander. What do you think about all this, as the Security officer who will look after Doctor Bulman?'

Smiling gently at her, despite the heat, he said: 'I think that it's very hot and I've been standing here a long time waiting for you mob to finish. I also think I'll take that mike and stuff . . .'

'Simon!' Bogie grabbed him by the forearm. 'Remember what Stacey said about putting on a front.'

The girl had retreated, frightened by the venom in his voice, contrasting with the pleasant smile on his face.

'Right, Bogie. The dreck looper on Golot Four was what he said, if I remember right. That's what he usually says.' He wiped sweat from his forehead, desperately wanting to get out

---

* For Simon Rack's early life, see *Simon Rack: Earth Lies Sleeping.*

of the constrictions of his number ones and take off. 'Razan? Nobody knows. Not that hard in the Federation to hide or change in some way. No record on fingers or sweat pattern or eyes. He hasn't allowed any Federation executive to go up there since he started five months ago. Each week another shuttle takes off from this port and takes never more than ten men and women up there. No visitors. They get frozen up there on a minimum of six months. No maximum. All very rich. Some very famous. He's convinced them it works, and that's all that matters. We've been told on this mission to keep our eyes and ears open, but above all to avoid trouble. Razan only lets us up there after a lot of fuss. I figure Bulman's such a big catch for him he's breaking his rule and we'll come back unfrozen.'

There was a hideous croaking noise next to Rack, like thick oil trickling down a slimy sump. One of the vid-pix men jumped back looking startled. Simon didn't move, having heard Bogie's laugh before.

Many times.

'I reckon Stacey really wanted to get us to go for the six months freeze, just to keep that secret safe. I think he was disappointed that Razan backed down in the end.'

The idea of the two of them being frozen away in tiny capsules for six months was so ridiculous that Bogie had another laughing fit.

Somehow, Simon didn't find it as funny. His sealed orders had contained provisions for exactly that happening. It had only been a last-minute decision for them to be allowed to come back on the next shuttle up.

In seven days.

A commentator for the local vid-station had come and positioned himself right at their backs, braying away excitedly at his mike to keep the watching millions clued in on what was happening. The weekly departures of the Paradise shuttle had come to be a top draw on the stations. There was something ghoulishly pleasurable in sitting in your cramped living cubicle and watching the unthinkably rich going off on a flight, knowing that you might never see them again. Men and women who had become household names throughout the known galaxy. Off to be frozen alive.

'Here they are, folks. Eight of the very, very best out of the topmost drawer on half a dozen worlds. The first coming away towards the ship after the formalities is business mogul, Rafael Strafford. Most of you must have eaten one of his instant foods. Mister Strafford, could we . . .?'

Face set, the big man pushed him aside without a word, climbing the short flight of steps to stand and wait by the door. His curly hair was nearly white, and lines of age showed on his black skin.

Undeterred by the snub, the reporter droned on: 'The elderly lady coming next is the famous artist Miss Angelika Wellcome. Some of her sonic sculptures decorate public buildings all over the . . . and here's Viki Laurel. And if you think I'm goin' to have to tell you about the deeelightful and utterly deeeloverly Viki, then forget it, boys and gals.'

In the world of vid, Viki Laurel was one of the biggest of all the lady stars. Beginning as a nudie extra in skin-flick exploiters, she'd made it to the top. The commentator was under orders not to stress the tragic reason that was taking the tall blonde up to Paradise. Even the finest medical minds had still not found a cure for leukaemia, and Viki's terminal illness had crowded all other news off the vid-screens for weeks. Now she was going. A goddess ascending to her own heaven in a golden chariot.

Draped in black furs, face hidden behind enormous shades, Viki was helped to the steps by her latest husband. Since the young man's channel wasn't the one that had paid for the exclusive last words, Viki contented herself with a soulful smile for the cameras, and a final wave for the crowds, following the frail figure of the lady artist up the stairs.

'In that so, so sad moment, we missed the next of the biggies. Star-sleddin' diplomat, Karl Von Neumann. He's kept us all in peace for so many years that . . . and here comes another familiar face to watchers of this channel. It's our own, our very own, Zeta Price.'

'Friggin' hesher!' hissed Bogie.

Zeta Price ran a news and gossip talk show eight times a week and told anything about anyone, picking on the easiest targets, and using the maximum exploitation techniques. He was a faded sixty, hair tinted silver and green, with a small, repulsively fat dog tucked under his arm.

'Bogie? I want you up the steps straight after Bulman. Once his foot's off the ground here, then he's ours. Right?'

'Oke,' replied Bogart, touching the hilt of his colt in its holster, making sure the stun button was on maximum depression. Bulman was way too important for any foul-ups.

With an excess of gushing and a final tearful hug, Zeta Price climbed the steps, mincing along awkwardly on his high-heeled silver and green boots.

Wiping away a manly pearl from his bronzed cheek, the linkman went on with his introductions. All boring stuff, swallowed in huge gobbets by his viewers. To Simon and Bogie, who'd been studying files on every member of the shuttle, there was nothing there they didn't know, though there was much they could have told that would have opened eyes.

Like about the Girondes. Rumoured to be the richest couple in the universe, with commercial interests in all sorts of things. Some public and some private. Like Colonel Stacey said when they reached them in the briefing: 'Wallace and Ruth Gironde have their dirty fingers in all the dirty pies going. Girls, boys, dope; you name it and they've got vested interests there. Wallace is reputed to be in his nineties, maintaining a fragile hold on life only through an assortment of pacemakers and other artificial aids that keep his own organs functioning. Ruth was a "model",' Stacey stressed the word with suitable scorn, 'in one of the Gironde establishments way back. Before he met her and made her the eleventh wife.'

And there they were. The old, old man being winched up on the lift to join the others at the locked doors of the gleaming shuttle craft that would soon whisk them away to Paradise. Ruth slapped at the vid interviewer and rushed up to join her husband. Both Bogie and Simon were in close and both saw the lines of tension round the eyes and mouth. They looked at each other.

'Trouble,' mouthed Simon, and Bogart nodded his agreement. While most of them were embarking as though they were looking forward to their chance of immortality, Ruth Gironde looked more as though she were on her way to attend her own execution.

'Here's our man.' Bogie slipped away from Simon's side, eyes flicking nervously round the port, hoping that the boys up in the crowd were doing their stuff and that the nearby roofs were well covered. This was always a high-tension moment with important people. The time when some security guards got careless.

Early in their career as a lethal fighting team with GalSec they'd been back-up to a bodyguard duty on the head of state of a frontier world out in the questionable area of space. After a hazardous flight with three attempts on the man's life, they'd got to the spaceport, and everyone relaxed. Everyone except the assassins. Using vibroes they picked off the front team, breaking them apart, and would certainly have slain their target if Simon hadn't got them both with his blaster from the door of the ship.

'And here's the man we've all waited to see. The man whom those two excellent GalSec operatives are here to protect. They'll stay with him for every moment while he's up in Paradise, and they'll be with him at the last moment when he slips into the cold land where there are no dreams, and yet where

14

there will be an awakening. Perhaps millennia after you and I are timeless dust.'

Walking slowly, the lines of pain from the terminal disease carved deep, came Doctor Isaac C. Bulman. A name that few people had ever heard of and a face that had only leaped into prominence in the last month. After his shattering statement to the official Federation news bulletin.

Bogie never wanted to be involved in the background to their cases and hadn't bothered to plough through the sheaf of notes they'd been given on the man. All he wanted to know was what Bulman looked like and what they had to do to keep him safe. Nonetheless, Simon always tried to fill his partner in on the missions. Which was fine, as long as he kept it simple.

'Bulman's a genetic engineer. He plays with bugs, to find new ones that might be useful. Federation backing and tight controls. But there's always the risk of a rogue microbe coming out. Even more than one. They say that what's killing him is the result of an experiment that didn't work out right for him. And now he's off to Paradise.'

'Best place for him. These drecks who are always trying to save humans and forgetting about humanity.'

'Right, but he's done valuable work in helping clear new worlds and make them habitable. He was involved in that mission on Aleph.* Now it's over and he wants to go out quietly on Paradise, hoping that in a few years someone'll have come up with a cure for what he's got.'

'So? Why us? I've never seen Stacey looking so worried.'

'One little gold capsule is why, Bogie. Something that Bulman has been carrying with him for the last eighteen years, like a portable conscience. From the way I hear it, it's about two centimetres square, and it contains a single sentence. A simple formula for an exercise in genetic engin-eering that he stumbled on years ago as a side-effect of a chain

* For the story of this mission, see *Simon Rack: Starcross.*

of experiments. Bulman claims that anyone could memorise it and use it but he's never destroyed it.'

'A superbug?'

'Sort of. It breaks down the reproductive system of any organism and renders it permanently sterile. Bulman has always thought that it might be useful in controlling population.'

Bogart had interrupted him at that point, casually wiping on his trousers something he'd just excavated from his cavernous nostrils. 'Wait a minute, Simon. If it's that useful, where's the harm?'

'It doesn't just render you sterile. It also kills you within an hour. It's invisible. Tasteless. Can be put out as a gas or in liquid or as tablets. Bulman says it's potentially the most lethal organism he ever came across. And by God, he knows what he's on about.'

'So, at the last minute, we guard it and he gives it to us and we take it back to base? Easy. What's the risk?'

Simon scratched his forehead. 'Bulman's a scientist, and he's very naïve. If he'd just taken it with him in his memory, nobody could have got at it. But he *is* absent-minded and he's worried he might forget. Then he tells the world he's off to Paradise, with this bloody capsule. Hidden somewhere on him. Won't say where. Promises to give it to accredited agents of the Federation in his last moments before the ice hits the fan.'

Somehow, as he followed the spare figure of the geneticist up the stairs, Simon couldn't help feeling that he'd wasted his time trying to explain any of the subtleties of the mission to Bogie the day before. It might have been easier to have said that Bulman had a secret and that someone might try and get it from him. It was their job to look after him. After all, that was what it came down to. Saving a life, and maybe saving millions.

Made a change from killing all the time.

*　　　*　　　*

The crowd surged forwards, breaking the security lines, shouting and waving at their idols, particularly at the blonde Viki Laurel and the gaily-clothed Zeta Price. His dog became frightened at the noise and started yapping furiously. Simon turned to face the mob, keeping the party behind him. His hand rested easily on the butt of the blaster, ready to draw it at a moment's notice if things looked like getting out of hand.

But the guards had reasserted their control and the thin grey line was holding. The door of the shuttle ship slid open with a faint hiss and the rich began to file inside for their last trip to Paradise. Bogie stood by Simon at the top of the steps, looking down at the rippling sea of faces. Many of the women there were weeping at the thought that they might never see their beloved idols again.

'Phew! Wouldn't like to fall into that lot of maniacs. Be glad to get back into space.' He looked down at his wrist kron. 'Running late, Simon. Let's go.'

Apart from that minor temporal hitch, things were going smoothly according to the script.

But there's always someone who doesn't want to play the game to the rules.

The explosion of the blaster among the crowd was a unique and distinctive noise. The crack of power, sounding flat among so many people, was enough to snap round both Simon and Bogie. Although neither of them were aware of it, both had their own colts out in a fraction of time. Eyes searching for who had fired. They didn't have to look for long.

There was a ripple in the mob, like the underwater movement of some leviathan, and suddenly there was a space, with two bodies lying on the gleaming stone of the port. Men and women were fighting and yelling, trampling over each other as they tried to get away from the epicentre of the disturbance.

At the top of the shuttle steps, there were only three of the party left with Simon and Bogie. The tall Viki Laurel, the tiny Zeta Price, and the unworried figure of the black businessman, Rafael Strafford.

'Get inside,' snapped Rack, still trying to see who it was that threatened his mission. Holding his puppy to his skinny chest, the little man scampered into the safety of the metal hull. The girl and the man remained outside, watching curiously. They weren't included in Simon's brief, so he let them stay. If they wanted to get zapped, then that was their worry.

'You rotten bastards!!!! Damn you!!!!' The voice was thin and high, rising above the thunder of the crowd's panic like a gull over the roar of surf. At last they saw him. A small man, dressed in faded blue overalls, like thousands of other workers on Crucis, a dented blaster clutched in his right hand, walking unsteadily towards them. The security men behind him watched, frightened of shooting at him in case they hit any of their colleagues on the other side of the arc of fire.

Crouched down, holding their guns in the right hands, wrists steadied by their left hands, Simon and Bogie watched him come on. When he was within a few paces of the bottom of the steps, Simon shouted to him.

'Far enough, mister. Throw that down, and push the hands up. Else I'll take you out.'

'Think I care?' said the little man, ripping his overall top open. 'See that?' 'That' was a row of pale yellow sticks, strapped round his body. 'One shot and all that lot go up. I don't care what happens to me, now that Marylou's gone. I just want to stop this stinkin' ship from takin' these stinkin' rich bastards from goin' up to Paradise. When I knew Marylou was dyin', I went to them and begged them to take her. But they just laughed and sent me away. Even called the greys to come and take me out and threaten me with rehab.'

At his back, Simon was conscious of the warm breath of the lovely vid star on his neck. Soft as a summer breeze, she whispered in his ear. 'Kill him, Commander. Tear him apart now, while he's standing there. He's asking for it.'

Without even turning round, Simon reached behind him and pushed the idol of a galaxy in the face with the flat of his hand, sending her sprawling on her backside in the shuttle. She squeaked her dismay, but he ignored her. There was a quiet laugh from Rafael Strafford.

On the runway of the port, the little man still stood staring up at them. 'Just because I had no credits. That's what buys you life here. Credits. Don't matter Marylou been a good woman and leaves us with a passel of kids. Now she's gone and I'm alone.'

'What about your children, mister? Think you're helping them by doing this?'

The narrow eyes opened wider and looked directly at-Bogart. 'They don't care either. I sent them off to paradise after their mother. Just this morning. All of them. Only me left, and I'm goin' soon. I'm just here so folks know what drecks all these rich people are. I'm going to walk right up and shoot myself and send this whole ship up and all of you bastards with it. Then I'll be with Marylou and the kids again. So if you try and shoot me first, you'll be doin' just what I want. So I win, don't I? Hey, you up there. Tell em' I won.'

As carefully as if he were shooting targets at the training school range, Simon fired, hitting him clean between the eyes, sending the corpse crashing to the stone take-off bay.

'You lost.'

TWO

END OF MISSION – BEGINNING OF MISSION

'I was sorry that you had to kill that man, Commander.'

'I didn't enjoy it, Mister Strafford, but he wasn't leaving me a lot of room to manoeuvre.'

A frail, trembling voice came from the other side of the shuttle's main lounge, where all of the Paradise trippers were gathered. 'Was there not a great danger that the poor fellow might have blown us all up when you shot him?'

Simon turned to face Angelika Wellcome, still pale after the launching ordeal. He was disappointed to find that the ship was being run totally on auto, as a couple of lady stewards would have been a help.

'No. Not unless he'd done what he threatened and fired his blaster into himself at close range. When he showed me the explosive, I recognised it.'

'Yep,' interrupted Bogie. 'Pale yellow like that, it had to be a Pynazoxil base. Safe as houses, as long as it doesn't get either a proton charge or a hell of a bang from close up. You could hit it with a hammer and it wouldn't blow.'

'Serves him right,' sniffed Viki Laurel, still gazing out of the rear viewer at the silver dot that was Crucis.

'And so say all of us, dearie,' threw in Zeta Price. 'Poor little Humphrey here was quite, quite sick with terror over it all.'

'I am delighted to hear that it was only your animal that was so affected,' said Von Neumann, in a sarcastic voice that was quite wasted on Price.

The only members of the party missing from the gathering

were the Girondes. The old man had been taken ill in the excitement, and had retired to their small cabin with his wife to rest. The shuttle was excellently equipped with every conceivable medical device, and Simon hadn't the least doubt that Wallace Gironde would make it to Paradise and the chance it offered him for a second chance at life.

The man they were there for, Isaac Bulman, sat silent and alone in a corner of the elegant room, thumbing through a notebook. He hadn't once commented on the incident at the spaceport.

'How much longer before we get there?' The question, asked in the querulous whine that seemed his common mode of speech now he was away from his image on the vid-screens, hung in the air. Price was forced to repeat it. 'You! I asked you a question! When do we get there?'

With studied calm, Rack turned and glanced at the much smaller man. Price had once done a hatchet job on the operations branch of GalSec, specifically mentioning an operation in which both Simon and Bogie had been involved. A nasty multiple kidnapping, which ended up with most of the girl victims dead.*

Price had exposed them on his vid-show, making them appear incompetent buffoons. Simon hadn't forgotten that quickly, even though Zeta obviously had.

'Are you talking to me?'

'Of course. Who else?'

Bending down, Simon grabbed him by the front of his tight-fitting jacket and pulled him to his feet. 'Listen to me, you jumped-up little snot. Up here you are a nothing and a nobody. You want to make it to those freezing capsules in one piece, then you change your tone and start using words like "Please" and "Thank you". Is that clear, Price?'

The little man gazed frantically round the lounge, tugging at the collar of his immaculate suit, where some of the hand

* See *Simon Rack: Planet of the Blind*.

embroidery had come unpicked. But everyone was either looking away, or showing what they thought of him. His pro-
grammes, with him as a prophet of doom, might have brought
him top ratings for years, but they hadn't left him many friends.

Shaking his head at the angry and impotent Price, Karl von
Neumann spoke softly. 'We agree with the Commander, you
silly little person.'

Lips white, eyes like a snake, Price stood up, snatching his
dog. 'I'm not in my ice yet, folks. I can still do something for
you. For all of you.'

And he walked out, the automatic doors sliding noiselessly
shut after him. For the first time, Bulman looked up and spoke.
'He is a walking proof that there is no honour in being a
prophet. In your own or in any country. And if you will all
forgive me, I shall go to my room. Commander, I believe we
will dock at Paradise in,' he consulted a black digital kron on
his slender wrist, 'about forty-seven hours. Is that not so?'

Simon nodded. 'Right, sir. Ensign Bogart will come with you,
if you don't mind, and keep watch outside your door. I'll spell
him after four hours.'

Bulman smiled his appreciation, and got up, a momentary
pang of pain checking his movement. Watched in silence by
the others, he went out.

Grinning happily at Simon, Bogie marched smartly out after
him. Both GalSec men were in their working rig, having grate-
fully changed out of their number ones even before the shuttle
had lifted off.

Bogie reckoned that this was going to be an easy mission.
Rightly, he'd guessed that there might be trouble at the lift-
off. But with a double handful of some of the richest and most
powerful people around, he couldn't see any trouble.

The night after their briefing, when they'd gone through
the files on the passengers, he'd laughed at the idea that any
of them would bother to steal Bulman's deadly secret.

'Why the hell should they? They've got everything they

22

want. All of them. And they're going to get something that no other person in the galaxy is getting. A second chance of life. With all that, why risk it for a bit more? It wouldn't make sense.'

Simon had answered him, saying: 'They all might have everything they want. But they'd all be happy to have that little bit more.'

At mid-day the internal loudspeaker crackled and a smooth voice came over. 'This is Abraham Razan, welcoming you on behalf of Floyd Thursby Enterprises to the road to Paradise. In just twenty-four hours you will be with us. I look forward to that moment. Until then, may you fare well.'

The tone was unbelievably rich and soft. Bogie whispered to Simon that it was like rubbing the inside of a woman's thigh with a piece of black velvet. Since he wasn't normally given to poetic thoughts like that, Simon realised what a deep impression the voice of Razan had made.

The speaker clicked off. The ship continued to thrust its way on through deep space, towards the massive rotating station that was called Paradise. Many of the travellers were doped up on tranks, sleeping away the millions of miles. Turn-and-turn-about, Simon and Bogie carried out their duties, guarding Bulman, going with him everywhere. During their rest periods, they also slept.

There was nothing else to do.

Until later that afternoon – although time ceases to have a deal of meaning on that sort of trip, one still generally uses the time system of the planet that has just been left. So back on Crucis, it was late afternoon. On the shuttle, it was less than a day until they reached their golden destination.

Simon was sleeping, still fully dressed, in one of the tiny cubicles that the ship provided. Bogie was on watch in the corridor at the other end of the shuttle, where he could watch Bulman's sleeper. The steady vibration of the grav-comps made sleep easy, lulling the body.

The previous day, when he'd been asleep, he'd been abruptly woken by a scream from the room next door that had brought everyone on the ship running. It had been Viki Laurel, trying to come down off some sort of trip that she'd got into before they even took off. Simon had been the only one of them who'd actually heard what she cried out, and it had given him a sharp insight into the life of an inter-galactic vid-star.

Viki's voice had been anguished beyond belief, torn from the dark side of the soul where only nightmares dwell. Each word seemed to be ripped from her throat, ragged-edged. He'd got in before the others, colt in hand, and had seen the taut mask of horror drawn tight over her lovely face. Heard those agonised words repeated in a whisper. 'Please don't make me! Not with all of them! !'

This time the tranks were working and Viki Laurel had been sleeping easily. There was a soft rapping on the plasteel door of his cubicle, like a gloved hand scratching for entrance. Simon swung his boots off the bunk, hand going as an automatic reaction to the blaster in his belt, although few killers came knocking at the door.

Few did, but Simon had known some who had, and even known men who'd died from not believing it.

'Who is it?'

'Me. Ruth Gironde.' The voice, with its faint twang that told of a Sol birthplace, was pitched so quietly that he could barely catch it. He opened the door, and the woman slipped quickly in, pushing it shut herself before he could move.

Ruth Gironde was a fine-looking lady. Tall, coming close to Simon's height, wearing a loose gown of some kind of clinging skin in light amber with orange highlights. Her black hair was loose over her shoulders, held only with a single clasp of diamonds. The skin was flawless, apparently unmarked by any kind of contact with reality. Full lips, partly open, showing immaculate teeth beneath. White and seeming to Simon to be

24

slightly pointed like a carnivorous animal.

But the eyes! Whites as pure as snow on a mountain peak. Irises a uniquely deep purple. Simon had seen eyes of all colours, even patterned, but that always meant contax. Even with the micro ones, you could always tell them up close, and he was very close to Ruth Gironde. That purple was real. Eyes that a man might easily drown in, they were so deep and so beautiful.

They were also terrified. The eyes of someone who was nearing the bottom of the pit and could see no hope of ever climbing out again.

The sleeper only held the bunk and a small chair. Simon stood back, without speaking, and waved her to the chair, while he perched uncomfortably on the edge of the bed. 'Mrs Gironde? Is anything wrong?'

Something obviously was, but he instantly realised that he'd asked the wrong question.

'Wrong?' The word was loud, almost a shout. 'Wrong! Is anything wrong. Krishna!! What a question, Commander. Why not ask me what's right, and I can tell you in a single word. Nothing. Nothing! Nothing!!'

She began to laugh. The brittle thin laughter of hysteria. Whatever it was, Simon didn't want his career ruined by old man Gironde coming hobbling in after his screaming wife and finding her in his cubicle. Wallace Gironde had an awesome reputation for guarding all of his possessions, and that had always included his wives.

He reached out and slapped Ruth across the face, hard enough to knock her head back against the bulkhead and stopping her laughter like turning off a tap. The marks of his fingers stood out redly on her white skin, like a macabre birthmark.

She rubbed at the mark with her long fingers, and then smiled wearily at him. 'Commander, I suppose this is where I'm supposed to say "Thank you, I needed that." Well, nobody needs a slap in the face, but I'm grateful for your quickness. It would not have been pleasant for us . . . for either of us, if Wallace had come in here.'

Simon smiled back. 'I sort of figured that, Mrs Gironde. He is a well-known man, you know.'

'Call me Ruth, Commander. It's Simon, isn't it? Do you mind if I call you Simon while we're on our own? It seems so much less formal and more friendly.'

'That's okay with me, Ruth. But you came here for something. Just to be friendly?'

She crossed her legs, exposing an immoderate amount of creamy thigh. Simon and Bogie had been away on a niggling mission on a frontier world for some weeks and any leave owing to them had been stopped by Stacey for what he described as overstepping the regs. That meant they'd had to lean on a dealer in undesirable items, and he'd crumpled up like a wet tissue. It turned out he'd had a weak heart for years. The mission had ended reasonably, but they'd drawn this one without even a forty-eight to relax.

Looking at Ruth's legs, Simon reckoned back and found it had been nearly six months. That was too long. Now here he was cramped in a small room with the beautiful wife of one of the most powerful men in the galaxy. Ruth Gironde had been a society lady for several years before meeting Wallace, and being wooed and won by him. There was no threedee vid on top people complete without some item about Ruth Gironde. She was the galaxy's first lady. Infinitely desirable, and infinitely unattainable.

So they said.

Outside was the limitless cold and nothingness of space. Ahead of them, coming closer all the time, was the station of Paradise, closed to all but the most privileged few. Inside the shuttle it was very quiet. The auto-pilot made the necessary

26

minute corrections needed to their flight pattern, silently guiding them on course.

There were only three people awake. At the far end of the ship, Ensign Bogart leaned against the wall, and amused himself with a tiny liquid flow puzzle in black and silver he'd picked up at the Crucis port. There were still over two hours before he was due to be relieved. The thought of relief made him conscious that he hadn't gone to the crapper before taking over from Simon. He glanced up and down the short corridor, wondering whether he dare risk slipping away. Much as he and Simon hated discipline, neither would dream of risking a mission by idleness, or carelessness, and he sighed and went back to playing with the puzzle.

Down the other end of the shuttle, Ruth Gironde leaned back in the chair, nibbling at the ragged corner of skin on an index finger, just below the chromed nail.

'Why have I come, Simon? If I had till the end of time, I couldn't even begin to tell you all about it.'

Simon swung his feet back on the bunk, making himself comfortable. 'Come on, Ruth. Try me.' He couldn't wipe out an odd feeling of unreality that here he was actually calling the mythical Ruth Gironde by her first name.

'Well. You know I'm younger than Wallace?'

That was like saying that a newborn baby was younger than its grandfather. Simon simply nodded.

'The only thing that keeps Wallace alive is that collection of machines he carries around with him. His heart is so bad that even the merest shock could wipe him off. You saw what happened at the port with that maniac with the gun? He's got over that, but his doctors have been telling him for months that he could go at any time. That's why Paradise was such a gift for him. It gives him a chance for another time round. By the time he's revived, there might be ways to bring back the youth he lost . . . eighty years ago.'

There was a depth of bitterness to the girl's voice that got through to Simon. Even from what she'd said already, he was beginning to get a clue as to what was really wrong with her. Before guessing at it, he let her talk it out some more. That seemed to be what she wanted.

'That's it, Simon. He needs to die. He's old, old, old!' There was horror in the way she repeated the word. Looking at her — at her slim body. The firm breasts, warm thighs. The ebullience of her youth.

'When I married him, I was fond of him. Truly fond. He was a great man. One of the most powerful men of our time, and he flattered me. Promised me anything. I believed him. Once I was his, he locked down on all the doors. I never saw anyone whom he didn't want me to. He has few friends. All old men. And that was my life. A rich bird in a cage of diamonds.'

She began to weep softly to herself. Simon got up and stood by her, resting his hand nervously on her shoulder, feeling her body shaking with loneliness and grief. She reached up and took his hand, pressing it to her cheek, so that he could feel the wetness of her tears. Without speaking, Simon took her by the hand and led her to the narrow bed, pulling her beside him. Ruth tucked her head into the crook of his neck and carried on talking, the sobs gradually easing away.

'Now he wants me to join him in a long trip into eternity. And I don't want to go.' There. That was what he'd suspected. But after the earlier screaming, the words were delivered quietly and resignedly.

'Why go, then? You're free. He can't make you. If he tries then we can stop him and you can come back with us.'

She rolled over on her side, looking crookedly up at him. 'You're sweet, Simon. Like him.'

'Him?'

Ruth Gironde shook her head, closing her eyes as though she were very weary. 'No. I can't tell you his name, Simon. Wallace would somehow find out. Just someone I met a year or so back and I fell in love with him. He was young and strong and everything that Wallace isn't. In fact he was even very poor. He loved me back, and then Wallace found out. There isn't anything he can't find out if he wants. The houses are all packed with his bugs and sniffers and spies. He found out.'

Her body was very close to him, her breasts pressing against his chest. Gently, like trying to pick a butterfly off a meadow flower, Simon put his fingers to her body, and began slowly to caress her. He felt the tips of the breasts immediately stiffen at his touch, and she moaned a little under her breath.

'Oh, Simon. It's been so long. Since . . . His white body. Pale, like a slug you kick up in a garden under a large wet stone. Wrinkled and soft and impotent.' She shuddered, and Simon put his arms right round her, squeezing her against him. Her fingers feathered over his face, down his neck, and rubbed his chest.

'The things I had to do to try and give him the satisfaction he still remembered! He was inhuman.'

'What happened when he found out about you and . . . this other man?'

'If he'd killed me then. Or even if he'd killed . . . him. If he'd done it then, I could have coped with it. But he told me he knew, and that he had "made arrangements" to ensure that I never saw him again. He hadn't wasted him. I thought he had. He kept him prisoner on one of his estates, giving him enough to keep him alive. There was a doctor there, skilled in mutating things. He showed me pictures of what he could do to my lover. Turn him into an obscene mewing parody of a man. Unless I did what I was told to. Then he would live and be well looked after.'

'He's still alive? How do you know?' His hands were roaming lower on her body, exploring the slit in the dress, and finding her naked beneath it. Her flesh was warm and responsive. In turn, she let her hand slip lower between them. Until she touched him, stroking him as he responded to her.

'Wallace thought of that, like he thinks of everything. He knew his hold would be gone if he died, so he kept getting new vids and threedees and tapes made of him and making me watch them. While I watched them, he used to make me . . . do things for him. He's sick, Simon. Old and sick, but not senile. He enjoys his revenge every day. His last joke was to insist that I share his cryogenic trip. Then we can wake together.'

'Why didn't you kill him?' To Simon it was the obvious and simple solution.

She didn't answer for a moment, concentrating on helping him wriggle out of his uniform trousers. Insistently she pulled him to her, guiding him into her. Simon gasped at the heat and wetness of her, gripping him and seeming to suck at him with a passionate ferocity. He began to move his hips against her, grinding her under him.

'That's good, Simon. Ooooh, Krishna, that's so good. Slowly now. Touch me. No, there. Yes. Yes. Deeper! Deeper! Hard, Simon. I want . . . Yes!'

After, Simon lay back spent, feeling as though he'd gone into warp without the grav-comps working. Once the act was complete, it was a characteristic of his that he couldn't take anything seriously for a time. It even crossed his mind that Ruth Gironde might not have been the best lay he'd ever had. Not quite! But she was certainly the most expensive.

Although he'd never be able to tell anyone about it – not even Bogie – there was a desperate desire to boast of how he laid the wife of the richest man in the galaxy, with her husband asleep only a few metres away.

In turn, she was sleepy and contented, seeming happy just to lie there, her hand resting on his body, eyes closed, and mouth slightly open.

'That was wonderful, Simon Rack. You asked me why I didn't kill Wallace. Because my lover would die within minutes. As soon as the word got back. I have to go through with it.'

She kissed him on the mouth, the tip of her tongue probing at his lips, sucking his tongue into her mouth, so that he could taste the sweetness. And the hint of corruption?

'Again? Once again, Simon. Once we are on Paradise, then there will be no chances. Let me go to the caskets with the taste of a real man on me, and the feel of a real man between my thighs. Please.'

It was an offer that no man would have been able to refuse. The second time, their coupling was slower and more gentle, with less of the urgency and ferocity of the first loving. Although the temperature on the shuttle was comfortable, Simon felt sweat trickling down his back and chest, making the movements of their bodies slippery. As she reached her climax, Ruth Gironde cried out softly in her passion. Cried out a name.

Not her husband.

Not Simon.

Afterwards, they dressed quickly and awkwardly in the confined cubicle. Outside, Simon thought he heard someone moving, and he froze, fingers reaching for the colt, but the noise stopped and he couldn't even be sure if he'd imagined it or not.

Before she left, Ruth came close to him, and held his hand, brushing his cheek with her lips, smiling sadly. 'It was very good, Simon. Thank you. If there's anything? I have a great deal of . . .'

'No.' Simon hushed her by putting his finger to her lips. 'There's nothing. The best things to keep are memories. They never grow old or stale.'

She nodded quickly, looking down at the floor. Simon thought of all her wealth and power and saw what it had brought her.

'Ruth? Why did you come here today? Was it just to have someone to tell. So somebody would know?'

Her hand already on the catch of the door she turned again

31

to face him. 'How old are you, Simon Rack?'

'Nearly twenty-seven.'

'Very young. Nearly the same age as I am. You're very wise, Simon. Keep that. Yes, I wanted somebody to know.'

'That was all?'

She smiled at him, and he was stunned by the radiance of her beauty, and saw what had tempted the ageing Wallace Gironde. 'No. That wasn't all I came to you for. And you gave me everything I could have wanted. And even a little bit more.'

She put her fingers to her mouth and blew him a kiss, then slipped out into the silent and deserted corridor, letting the door slide to behind her. It was several minutes before Simon glanced down at his kron and saw that it was nearly time for him to relieve Bogie.

The ship was still, apart from the ceaseless vibration of the grav-comps, providing them with a liveable level of gravity. The earliest experiments had proved that it was not possible for most people to endure weightlessness without serious mental and physical effects.

The sleeping cubicles were at the ends of the shuttle, separated by the central lounge. Simon walked quickly through it, whistling quietly to himself. Turned the angle towards where Bulman slept, and stopped dead.

Sprawled across the corridor, hands outstretched and empty, lay Eugene Bogart. The door of the cubicle beyond him was open. Simon stepped as softly as though he were walking on eggs, the blaster probing at the stillness before him, ready to face anything. Or anybody.

As he reached him, Bogie stirred, moaning quietly, fingers flexing, scratching at the floor. Simon ignored him, seeing the clot of blood on the back of the head where he'd been zapped, knowing from experience how hard that head was. There was something more important.

The moment he jumped into the small cubicle, colt ready,

Simon saw the truth. Isaac C. Bulman wasn't important. Not any more.

It had been done with a knife. Maybe an old-fashioned razor, with a needle edge. They were still used on some outback worlds. Whoever had done it had crept up on Bogie while he was on guard and slugged him from behind. Walked in and cut Bulman's throat without even waking him. The eyes of the dead geneticist were open, but the expression on his face was that of someone wakened from a short nap by some minor irritation. Not the face of a man brutally slaughtered. Perhaps the sting of the blade as it cut through the arteries under the left ear had just penetrated his mind.

A long way too late. The body was still relaxed and warm. Simon remembered the steps he'd heard while he was with Ruth Gironde. That must have been it.

He was tempted to press the panic button and get everyone running, but he saw the futility of it. Whoever had done it had chosen a time with nobody around, and would now be safely back in their own cubicles, all trace of the murder hidden or disposed into the shuttle vaporiser.

'What the . . .?' Bogie had come round, and was leaning in the doorway, holding his head. 'Jesus H. Christ! That blows it, Simon.'

Apart from the spurt of blood on the ceiling and wall by Bulman's head, there was comparatively little mess, with most of the blood soaking into the bunk and being absorbed by the blankets.

Stepping back from checking the heat of the corpse, Simon felt something grind under his heel and bent down to pick it up. Holding it out wordlessly on his palm to Bogie.

It was a small capsule. Gold. About two centimetres long. Open.

And empty.

The news had been transmitted back to GalSec base, causing

the panic that Simon had expected. What he didn't expect was that there was no recall order. Just to carry on to Paradise and try to recover the missing information before the seven men and women took the long journey.

Simon went through the motions of interrogating everyone, but it was a waste of time, with them all telling the same story. They'd been in their bunks, and they'd heard nothing. Two of them were lying. Simon knew that.

Ruth Gironde had been with him. And the killer had been loose on the shuttle.

Afterwards, with Paradise only a couple of hours away, they talked in Simon's room over what had happened. A close search of the ship had revealed nothing. Except the charred remnant of a strip of paper in the corridor near the door to Bulman's room. Useless to them, except to tell them that the killer now had the genetic information committed to his memory.

'In that case, we can monitor all transmissions from the station. If nothing goes out, then it'll freeze with the killer. No problem.'

Simon shook his head. 'You amaze me, Bogie. Don't you ever look further than the end of your nose? What about when they get thawed out? Say in only six months. They'll still have the information.'

Bogie's homely face lit up with another idea. 'Waste them all and get out in a lifeship. That way it's safe.'

'No.' Simon scratched his head. 'It's a good idea, and I have thought about it. But it's risky. Blowing something like this, with all this crowd on, is a bit drastic. And dangerous.'

'And?'

'And there's no bloody lifeship. I checked.'

That ended that part of the talk. They ran through the members of the party, trying to guess at a reason for any of them killing.

'You can't say, Bogie. Some have obvious reasons, like more

power. Others might have reasons that you might not even begin to guess at.'

They had a rule as partners, that they would never break, that they told each other everything about their missions that might be important. Up till the killing of Bulman, Simon had intended to keep his brief affair secret from Bogie. Now it might be important, and he told him all about it. More or less all about it.

The response from Bogart was a mixture of surprise, envy and suspicion. The envy was leading by a mile, tinged with curiosity, when suspicion took over with a rush.

'A decoy! Keep you out of the way while I got zapped? Could be.'

Simon nodded, reluctantly. It could be. Whoever hit Bogie had been fast and vicious. If it hadn't been for the thickness of his skull, it could easily have been two murders. That seemed to rule out Angelika Wellcome, and Wallace Gironde. But either of them could be exaggerating their illnesses and infirmity. They couldn't rule either of them out.

'I somehow don't reckon it. No reason, Bogie, but you know I'm generally . . .'

'Sometimes,' interrupted Bogie with a grin. 'But the way you tell it, I don't see her either. Unless she figured to use the info to help get her lover out of old man Wallace's leathery hands.'

Their speculations were interrupted by the voice of Razan pouring smoothly out of the speakers. 'We will be welcoming you to Paradise within a very short time now. Please begin to make your preparations for disembarkation. The auto-pilot will give you final instructions when it is necessary. We all hope you have had a good trip and look forward to helping you enjoy the last seven days of your old life.'

Bogie grunted. 'Back at school they never told me the way to win paradise was with a few million credits.'

Simon thought back to the haunted eyes of Ruth Gironde. 'Maybe. For Ruth, I guess *that* paradise is already lost.'

35

THREE

COMING, GOING, COMING AND GOING

'Paradise is really heaven,' exclaimed Angelika Wellcome, as they stepped aboard the circular space station at the end of their journey.

Some of the others laughed, but there was a hushed note to it. Paradise really was very impressive. Everything that the ad. brochure had said it would be. And then some. The carpets they trod on were inches thick, caressing the feet and ankles. Fine tapestries hung on the walls, all chosen with exquisite taste. Sonic statues, including some of Angelika's best work, hummed and sang softly in the corners of the vast reception area.

White-coated assistants appeared from nowhere and the still-ailing Wallace Gironde was whisked away to the station's sick bay for treatment that would enable him to survive long enough to be frozen to life in seven days. Ruth hesitated, wondering whether to go with him, then decided to stay with the others. She hadn't even looked at Simon since the discovery of the corpse of Isaac Bulman.

The body had been removed from the shuttle with maximum discretion, vanishing somewhere behind the scenes to go into the Paradise vaporiser and be spread into space in millions of sterile particles. That was one of the contractual rules of the station. If anyone died there, or on the way there, their corpses would not be returned to earth for disposal. They would stay for ever in space.

Simon and Bogie had watched intently over the viewers as

the ship approached the station, trying to figure out its internal organisation. There were few clues from the shape and exterior layout. Circular, like most orbiting bases, with the characteristic shimmer from its meteorite deflectors. Two observation ports near the top and the entry for the shuttle.

About one hundred and fifty metres in diameter with starlight gleaming off its silvered sides as they slowly rotated. In some ways, Simon had expected an outward display of ostentation, with flashing lights and glowing signs saying 'Welcome To Paradise'. There was none of that. In fact, there was virtually no official welcome at all to Paradise. Just the assistants dealing with the dead and the dying, whisking off their luggage to their own cabins. Another rule was that nobody was allowed to bring more than two trunks to the station, and that, on their freezing, the contents of the trunks became the absolute property of Paradise. And Floyd Thurby Enterprises, the holding company based on Crucis.

The disposal of the passengers' assets had already caused problems among planetary courts, and there was a committee of Federation lawyers currently working on all the legal possibilities. Was the man or woman who had gone to Paradise to be frozen to be registered as dead? Or merely given the same status as a person injured and fallen into a coma? Paradise guaranteed to take care of all revival procedures, at the time specified on the contract. Some had chosen annual renewals. Mainly those with carcinogenic diseases. Others had picked a date a hundred years ahead. One man had even specified a thousand years. In cases like Wallace Gironde, his contract made it clear that he was only to be unfrozen when a cure had been found for all of his ailments – neatly listed on a separate sheet – *and* some method had been found for reversing the ageing process.

Like Bogie said: 'That could just be for ever.'

But time was on the side of these pampered rich. When a person was immersed in the freezing clouds, according to the brochure, time ceased. 'It is as though the client slips easily into a deep and dreamless sleep. Eons of eternity pass away like a summer morning. Seasons come and go. Civilisations may rise and fall. To the sleeper in his cocoon of Paradise, all that is as nothing. And on awakening . . . the spirit will be purged and bright and cleanly, ready to face every new challenge of a new world.'

Most of the passengers sat down on the deep chairs and loungers scattered round the reception area. Simon and Bogie chose to try and leave, to get a better idea of the surroundings. And instantly ran into a problem. Every door was locked. Not only locked but guarded by husky young men, armed with needle-blasters. Guns that were designed to control rather than kill. That would cause a reaction ranging from a tingling numbness in the part hit, to stinging pain and paralysis. In the hands of experts, a needle gun could also kill if it was aimed at the head.

'I'm sorry, Commander Rack. The orders of the Exalted Abraham Razan are quite clear and unambiguous. No man or woman leaves here until he has cleared them. He will soon be here. Why not take a seat and wait like the others?'

Without a word, the two officers turned and walked back to the centre of the room, standing near an intricate sonic sculpture of green crystalline form. Sensing the men's anger, it ceased its melodic crooning and began to whine and moan to itself. A reaction that annoyed Simon even more and he moved irritably away from it.

'This is going to be a heavy trip, Bogie. I can feel it in the vibes from those smooth bastards. Looks like Razan runs himself a mother of a tight ship here.'

'We got time, Simon. Play it very cool for a couple of days and then start leaning.'

'Seven days, Bogie. That's all. Then everyone you see here is going to be taken away and deep-frozen, and that'll probably be the last time we ever see them. And we have to quit on that seventh day.'

'So, we labour at it for six days, and on the seventh we'll . . .'

Bogart's philosophy was interrupted by a door sliding silently open at the rear of the lounge, and the appearance through it of the Exalted Abraham Razan. He was even more impressive in the flesh than in his threedee pic, towering over two metres tall.

He wore a loose gown of shimmering gold and silver, with a thread of black running through it. His hair was silver, long, pulled back behind his head in a gold clip. A necklace of what looked like enormous uncut gems dangled round his neck, the lights bouncing back off their dull surfaces. Despite his unbelievable height, he was also painfully thin, weighing, Simon guessed, not more than one-thirty pounds. His wrists were skinny, barely able to support the massive gold bracelets.

The face was equally distinctive. High forehead and prominent cheekbones swooping down to a thin-lipped mouth and a precipice of a jaw. The eyes were most peculiar, with the whites and the irises seeming to gleam with a silvery hue. Contax, almost certainly, thought Simon, unless it was due to some kind of disease.

The voice that had thrilled them on the shuttle was even more powerful, rounding out and filling the room, sounding as though he was speaking only to you.

'My dear, dear friends. I cannot tell you what inexpressible pleasure it gives me to welcome you today to Paradise. I heard with sorrow that there had been a going-before on the shuttle bringing you here.'

'It wasn't a going-before. It was a man with his throat hacked open.'

Simon grinned at the shocked silence after Bogart's words. Apart from the obvious truth of what Bogie had said, he knew why he'd chosen to phrase it in that deliberately shocking way.

It provided a healthy contrast to the phony dreck that Razan had been pouring out.

Unworried by the interruption, the lean giant smiled down at Bogart. 'I understand that you are concerned by the incident on your shuttle here.'

'Not as concerned as Bulman was.' Bogie was totally unworried by the opulent surroundings, and was clearly out to show it.

'Eugene, why do you not relax and let all of your tensions slip away?' Razan seemed to be finding it just a little bit irritating, and the mask of benevolence had slipped by a fraction.

'He prefers to be called Bogie. Not Eugene. And we want to talk to you in private as soon as possible and see around the rest of the station.' Simon moved towards the door, as though he expected the Exalted Leader of Paradise to follow him.

Simon was watching Razan carefully, and he saw him stand for a moment at the request, almost as though he were waiting for instructions. If he was, then who was really running the place? The mysterious Floyd Thursby? A man whom nobody in all of the Federation records had ever seen or spoken to. No trace seemed to exist anywhere throughout the galaxy that Floyd Thursby lived. Or had ever lived. He wondered if Bogie had noticed the hesitation.

When the reply eventually came, the voice was as round and convincing as before, but there seemed to be a new note to it. One of power and aggression. 'Commander. I fear that you and your wonderful assistant are not clear as to your function here on Paradise. The agreement with the highest echelons of government was that you should be allowed to come here and be our guests for a week. A privilege not extended to anyone before. That the importance of Doctor Bulman was such that he would hand over to you, at the moment that he went on to the new sleep, some secret. Sadly, he is no longer with us. Does that mean that you are now in possession of the elusive secret?'

'No. It doesn't. Whoever killed him also got the capsule. One of the men and women who have come here knows that secret.'

Razan again paused, seeming temporarily thrown by this news. Then he went on. 'In that case, Commander, it appears that our agreement no longer stands, and you and your partner will return by the same shuttle in which you came.'

That seemed to be that as far as he was concerned and he moved over to the rest of the party, the welcoming smile stitched back on his face. But it wasn't over. Moving faster, Simon stood directly in front of him, looking up into the silvery eyes.

'No way, brother. No way at all. A man's been murdered and information stolen that could cause incalculable harm to the free balance of power within the Federation. You don't just throw us our guns and say run. Nobody says that to us. We're here for that information, and we don't go back until we get it. If necessary, I'll stop the whole place from functioning and get men out here to ship you all back to Crucis.'

There was instant consternation from everyone, except the aloof Razan. Von Neumann strode up to Rack, his face blazing with anger. 'Young man! You try to pull something like that on us and I'll break you.'

Bogie casually pulled away from the group, unbuttoning the holster on his colt. But Simon was still well in control. He ignored the angry diplomat, and spoke directly to Razan. 'It isn't the least concern who these people are here. I would act the same way if they were a bunch of beggars on Golot Four. Murder is still murder. Theft is still theft.'

'You do not understand, my dear Simon. Please sit down and I'll do my poor best to make you comprehend exactly what the situation is.'

For a moment, the overwhelming beauty of the voice and the reasonable tone made Simon feel as though he was a little boy again, about to be lectured in the mysteries of the galaxy by an old uncle who was infinitely wise. Someone who knew that the things they were discussing were really over his head, but the man of wisdom would still try and make it clear for him. It *nearly* worked. But not quite. Simon saw the trap he was being led into. Something close to basic hypno techniques, practised by someone who was better at it than Simon would have believed possible.

'I'll stand. Go on.'

A flicker of annoyance crossed that perfect face, but the voice was unaltered. 'Very well, Simon, my dear friend. Whatever you wish. The facts are simple and unarguable. The original intention of Paradise was for it to be based on the surface of a planet. Crucis was the first choice. It was pointed out that we were, in effect, offering immortality, but only to those who could afford the high prices. There was the feeling that this admitted inequality might provoke major disturbances. Therefore, we were offered a small subsidy to move out into deep space for our operation. I hardly think that the Federation would want anything to interrupt the smooth running of Paradise. After all, they have no power to interfere here. You are here as our guests. And, like all guests, it is possible for you to outstay your welcome. The agreement was for seven days. For no longer and for nothing else. You will leave at once.'

'Seven days. As you say, Razan, the agreement was for seven days. We will keep to that, as I'm sure you will. Our purpose may still be fulfilled if we can trace what we want in that time. If not ...'

'If not then you will go. Very well, we agree to that. But there is one provision ...' He paused, as though something had just struck him. 'Two provisions. You will make no attempt to interfere with the running of Paradise, and that includes a total embargo on the restricted areas of the station. And you will not provoke any disturbances with our guests here. If there are complaints, then you will go earlier. They are here to pass seven days doing exactly what they want. That is our agreement with them. It will not be broken.'

It was the best he could hope for, and Simon agreed to it. There was altogether too much power and money at stake for him to act the way he'd have wanted. This time, he really had to play it very carefully. In any case, from what he'd seen already it was obvious that the 'guests' were not the sort of people he could take round a corner and beat over the head with his colt until they confessed.

'Good. Then we are once more at peace. Simon, you will be treated just as one of our other guests, and you too, Bogie. Everything you want shall be yours. You only have to ask. But you will not become a nuisance either to us or to anyone else. I trust you will enjoy your time here and live to tell of it. Come, this has made us tardy.'

The veiled threat was hardly veiled at all. Razan held all the cards and he made sure they knew it. This was going to be a tough mother. As they were being taken to watch the previous week's guests being frozen into eternity, it crossed Simon's mind that there was only one way to play it.

Very cool.

They were taken through a narrow corridor, wading through slushy piped organ music, past walls lined with perfect copies of some of the finest works of art. Before they went to watch the cryogenic process being carried out they were led by Razan, towering along at a stately pace with the diminutive Angelika Wellcome on his arm, around Paradise.

'Simon! This is everything that the ad. said. The amount of money invested in this doesn't bear thinking on. It must be billions of credits.'

The two men brought up the rear of the party, with Rafael Strafford. Viki Laurel and Zeta Price chattered on ahead of them, Humphrey sleeping fatly in his master's arms. Von Neumann stalked remotely after the Exalted Razan, face blank, locked in tight with his own thoughts.

'Ensign, if you consider the subsidy that I know to be supporting this project, and the amount that each of us has paid for this privilege of life again, then the display here seems only what you would expect.'

Bogie nodded to the businessman. 'Thank you, Mister Strafford. What about the staff here? Seems to me like they must be top paid men.'

Simon answered that one. 'You must have been sleeping through that part of the briefing, Bogie. All of the men up here are rehabs. Bad ones. Only fit for simple precon work. Do as they're told and ask no questions. No chance of them being got at by an outsider. Even if anyone wanted to. Razan's taken no chances.'

After the tour, Simon had a clearer picture of how things were laid out. But no more idea of how that knowledge might help. One of the guards had come up and whispered something to the Exalted Leader, speaking softly into his ear, while the giant patiently bowed low and waited. Yet again, Simon couldn't banish the thought that he was getting some kind of orders or instructions from a tran. Maybe an implant in the skull. If it was right, and he was a front, who in Floyd Thursby Enterprises was the back man? Floyd Thursby himself?

The line of thought was filed away at the back of his mind for later use. Abraham Razan was talking again to them, his immense arms spread wide as he told them that there was a slight delay in the freezing process, and that they were not quite ready for them yet. 'So I suggest, dear Brothers and Sisters, that you go to your rooms and rest for an hour. Then we will call you again. If you wish for anything . . . *anything* . . . please request it. We welcome a challenge to our resources.'

With a swirl of black and silver he vanished through a sliding door and a stolid-faced attendant took up his stance in front of it. Muttering quietly to each other, the guests filed back to their compartments. Vastly larger than those on the

44

shuttle, and furnished in the best of taste.

Simon and Bogie had been put in together, at their own request, and shut the door behind them with a mutual sigh of relief.

'Hum?' said Simon.

Bogie nodded, and they sat together on one of the beds, rocking slightly as their weight started off the vibrating unit. Anyone watching would have suspected that he was seeing a pair of heshers at their strange practices. They put their arms round each other, hugging tightly, while they took it in turns to put their lips to each other's ears. One would listen, humming noisily while the other spoke. Then they would change round. Despite the most sophisticated bugging devices, the old and tried technique was still the most effective to prevent a conversation being either lip-read or sniffed.

'Ship's circular,' began Simon, giving a breakdown on the layout of Paradise as they'd seen it, trying to guess at what they hadn't yet been allowed to visit. 'We saw all the rec rooms. Vids, gym, sex rooms, music, nostalgia library. We'll see the labs and cryogenic quarters in an hour. Crew must live in that end block, beyond the gym. Through where Razan said food quarters were. That means something like this.'

He got up off the bed, and walked into the washing space. As on all ships, water was recycled, and there were the usual facilities. Seemingly made of expensive metals, and delicately engraved, but still the same old washer and crapper. Using the surface of the mirror and some water, Simon sketched a plan of Paradise, naming each part in a whisper, while Bogie watched and hummed. When they'd filled it in to their mutual satisfaction, they reached the same conclusion.

While Simon hummed, Bogie whispered. 'Allowing for that part through there, off the lounge area, being the cryo bit, then all that back there must be the lab. part and private quarters. Those are where we don't get in. Right?'

Simon shook his head. 'That's where they don't want us to

45

get in. Different. We'll play along and keep a low profile, like they used to say.'

They walked out of the wash area, and lay on the beds, both wrapped in their own thoughts. Simon wondered what the chances were of finding the secret of the capsule. Or the man or woman who had it. It was an obvious possibility that it had already been handed on to someone on Paradise, but that somehow didn't feel right. It smelled of a one-person job pulled for some private reason. One of the things to check out was for how long anyone had arranged to be frozen. But that might not give a clue, as there were clauses in the contract for the period to be waived at the authorisation of someone else appointed by the guest.

Bogie was also preoccupied with his own thoughts – most of which included the beautiful Ruth Gironde. Not to mention the even lovelier Viki Laurel. When the voice came over the speakers, it woke him with a start. Simon hadn't slept at all.

They were all given long robes to wear while they were in Paradise. Bogie had resisted it, exclaiming in a loud voice that it might be all right for heshers, but he wasn't going to . . . But he did. Both he and Simon wore them with a belt, making sure that their colts were secure in their holsters. Razan had made a token objection to the weapons, but Simon was on safe ground, having checked out that blasters had been cleared in the original agreement with the Federation authorities.

In single file, like a decrepit line of children, the guests were led to the cryogenic wing of the station to witness their predecessors being frozen. The treble doors were all guarded by armed men, watching them alertly, paying particular attention to the two GalSec officers. Finally Razan opened a door that brought them into a long, narrow observation chamber. A row of seats were provided in front of a strip window.

All of the party were there including Wallace Gironde, his malevolent eyes raking everyone. His breath wheezed deep in his chest and Bogie, sitting next to the old, old man, was sure he could hear the clicking and whirring of all the prosthetic aids that kept Gironde alive. Ruth sat the other side of her husband, alongside Price. For once the vid personality had agreed to leave Humphrey behind in his cabin, to the obvious relief of both Von Neumann and Strafford, neither of whom could stand either the dog or its master.

Viki Laurel perched on her chair next to Simon at the end of the line, keeping up an undertone of stoned chatter. Simon found it unsettling that she was blatantly naked under the thin cloth of the gown, the filmy material drawn tight across her superbly sculptured breasts, the nipples prominent.

Razan stood behind them, watching, like some monstrous father over his brood. 'In that chamber below, we will see the dear Brothers and Sisters who have completed their time here and now leave us for a sleep that will lead to their great awakening. We will watch them embark on the craft as you in turn will be watched by others. In this way, you will realise the continuity that is Paradise and share the experience of immortality. Watch and be linked with their joy.'

The rich tones faded away, and the room was silent. Entranced by what was happening, Simon leaned forwards against the table, peering through the polished glass. He felt fingers brush his thigh and whipped round to look at Viki Laurel, but she was gazing blank-faced at the scene ahead of them. He wondered for a second if he'd imagined it, but he knew he hadn't. The response from his own body confirmed it for him.

'Who are they?' The harsh voice was Wallace Gironde, drawing breath between each painful word, like a man fitted with an artificial voice-box.

Razan gave them a quick breakdown on the men and women who had filed into the chamber in front of them. There were eight. Seven of them were big business operators of mixed ages. Five women and two men. Three had incurable diseases and the others were coming to combat old age. None of them were names that meant anything to Simon or Bogie, until Razan linked them to the areas of commerce where they had once operated, and they were immediately familiar.

The eighth member of the party was a young girl, and she was carried in by an attendant and laid in her place. She was the daughter of a Government leader of a near-by world, and had lain like this in an unbreakable coma for the last four years after an accident. Simon remembered hearing about her a week ago, before their current mission had even been mentioned. 'The Sleeping Princess', the vids had called her. Now here she was, to be frozen to await the kiss of life from some surgeon prince in an unguessable future.

One of the first questions that Rack had asked at the briefing was how the freezing worked. Stacey had thumbed through a thick file marked 'Paradise' until he'd come to the relevant passage. It hadn't been long, and it came back to Simon as he sat in his chair and watched the final preparations being made.

'All previous attempts to resuscitate after freezing have failed. It has not proved hard to restore frozen specimens to a form of life, but tissue damage and failure has been so devastating that there seems no possibility of cryogenics being used on humans for many years. However, from the evidence that A. Razan has presented to us, he may have found some new technique to circumvent tissue damage. He has totally refused us any access to his laboratories, nor will he discuss them in detail. The vids we have seen are convincing as far as they go.'

That was the key phrase: 'As far as they go.' They were edited vids of a man being frozen, showing standard tests for suspension of life. Then the same man being revived and talking normally. But, as Stacey pointed out, it could all be faked.

At first Simon had found it hard to see how Razan had managed to get so many of the top people to come along on such a doubtful premise. Then he spotted where it was so clever. It must work, he guessed, but it might be such a simple process that it would become available to all. And that was just what the Floyd Thursby Enterprise didn't want. It had to be exclusive so that it could be expensive. And it offered the exact thing that these men and women wanted. The one thing that all their credits had never given them before. New life for old!

'Now it begins. Watch in silence, if you please. Each of the travellers will be hearing only their favourite piece of music as they go under. During the next seven days, you too will be asked to suggest what it is you would most like to hear. And your favourite colour so that the filters can screen them in for you. There is no pain. It is just as though you were slowly falling asleep in your own beds.'

Through the speakers on the wall they could hear the faint mixtures of the music. Mostly pre-neutronic classics, with Sibelius and Wagner leading. A faint mist began to rise from ducts along the sides of each of the tables. Lights flickered and colours rainbowed over the walls and ceiling. Simon could hear someone praying. Viki Laurel pattering away at a Christian prayer that must have been culled from her far-off childhood. And Ruth Gironde quietly chanting a mantra until a harsh word from her husband silenced her.

Each of the outgoing guests had their own couch, and they lay back on it, eyes closed, hands folded across their breasts. The mist rose about them, thickening, obscuring what was happening. The sides of the couch rose up to form a capsule, rising higher. While they watched entranced, the science-fiction dream took flesh and became astounding fact.

Through gaps in the drifting fog of white crystals they saw the sides rise higher, curving up and in until the figures vanished. After about five minutes, the shells were complete and the mist faded away. Moving in total silence, more attendants walked in and wheeled away the sealed pods.

'And there they will sleep. Alive but resting from the cares and pain of this world. Until they wish to awaken again. Unharmed and whole they will rise again. Though the idea tampers with traditional religious thought, I ask you to put all that behind you and only believe in the resurrection that we offer here. The resurrection of the body in Paradise!'

It was a fine speech, finely delivered. If Abraham Razan really was only a front man, then whoever picked him had chosen well. He was superb, his voice rolling over them with the reassuring tones of a prophet of salvation. It crossed Simon's mind that cryogenics might not be a bad idea. He saw so much death and so much sadness that there were times he almost wondered if it might not be possible for him too to get . . . He put the idea from him and tried to turn his mind back to the problem of the murder. It wasn't easy.

At his side, Viki Laurel had collapsed in tears, resting her head on her arms, body shaking with the force of her sobbing. Farther along, he was surprised to see the diplomat also wiping tears from his pain-ravaged face and he saw the power of hope to men and women whose hopes had been taken from them.

'There is one more short demonstration for you to watch. Dear Brothers and Sisters, and you too, precious visitors, watch and listen. For I must remind you here that your contracts are totally irrevocable from the point of view of finances at this time. You may still change your mind after this, but it will mean total sacrifice of the credits already lodged as well as penalty clauses being invoked. A thing which we have not yet had to do. If you reverse your intentions now, there will be no penalty, although all your credits will be held by us. But more than that, you will permanently lose your chance with the fragile Lords of Life.'

Nobody moved or spoke. The chamber below them was now empty. Viki Laurel had regained control of herself and watched events with new interest. A single capsule was wheeled in, glistening with what seemed like frost. The attendants stood by it, quickly disconnecting various pipes and cables. Razan explained what was happening.

'As promised, you have the opportunity to witness a resuscitation. This young man, named . . .' he looked down at some notes '. . . Jerzy Kornelis, volunteered to be frozen some six months ago. He is being paid well for this. He has slept, and he will now reawaken. Some of our guests, despite all of our proofs, still somehow fear we will not be able to bring them round on the great day of awakening. This demonstration is to allay those fears. In a short time, we shall witness this young man back in full possession of all of his faculties. The life support systems are now being disconnected.'

Again a mist filled the other room, but this time it seemed to Simon that it was more like steam. One of the men in white was handling a sort of hose, directing a jet of something at the ice-encrusted capsule to clean it off. In less than a minute it was clear and they could all see that it was stencilled with the man's name and the date of freezing. Six months and two days ago.

The men vanished again and there was silence. Faintly they heard the reedy notes of music. A modern piece that Simon recognised all the GalSec ground crews had been whistling about six months ago. 'They are given the same music as when they go under the process so that they are convinced that they have only been away for the shortest of naps.' He laughed. 'Indeed, when two of these demonstration cases were brought back to the present, they would not believe that they had been in a state of suspended animation for six whole months.'

'Razan?' Simon asked a question that had been bothering him for some time. 'Why six months? Why not less time?'

Razan swayed over to him, looming above him, placing a claw-like hand on his shoulder. Simon tensed, feeling the unexpected power in the grip. 'My dear Simon. You security men must always know the answers. Do you not realise that sometimes the questions are more important. It is six months because it *has to be* six months. There is no other reason.'

Simon wondered. Wondered how much of a coincidence it was that the first group to visit Paradise had gone up there just under six months ago. That meant more than twenty parties, including the present one, with about nine each party. Any day now the first of those early guests might start wanting to be revived.

It was a nagging thought.

'Look. I'm sure I saw . . . Yes.'

Wallace squeaked out his excitement as the top of the capsule cracked open and the sides began to drop slowly down. Ruth Gironde suddenly got up and ran out, hands to her face. Her husband hardly seemed to notice she'd gone. Razan pushed a button and an assistant came in, took his orders and then followed the woman out.

'The strain and excitement,' muttered Razan, more to himself than to any of the others. 'This is often the most powerful moment.'

The sides dropped down and vanished, leaving the man stretched out in his white robe on the flat couch. His face was pale, but his chest was clearly moving. Whatever else the process did, it certainly didn't kill its clients. The man was young, almost a boy, with tight curly hair packed on a round head. The face was handsome. Almost pretty. Shoulders broad, waist narrow.

After a moment, his eyes flicked open and he looked around him in bewilderment. The speaker picked up his first words after six months of suspended animation. 'Am I still in Paradise? Has it started? It can't be over. Can it. I feel . . . I feel perfectly normal. Like I did a couple of minutes ago. What . . .?'

Attendants came in, faces blank, helping him up off the couch. He seemed a bit wobbly on his legs, but he was quickly standing with their help. All the time he seemed puzzled, asking for reassurance that he'd really gone and that nothing had gone wrong.

Only when Razan spoke to him through the sound link did he smile and wave, finally being led away. As soon as he'd gone, Razan asked them all to stand and follow him. 'We will now go to the lounge where you will all be able to question young Kornelis about his freezing experience.' He hesitated as a thought seemed to come to him unbidden, and then turned to face Simon. 'I fear that we cannot allow you and your Ensign to meet him. After all he has gone through, perhaps it would be better if he did not meet someone who might be hostile. You do understand, my dear Simon?'

'Of course. We'll go back to our room, and catch up on some lost sleep. That was very interesting.'

Bogie was amazed at the ease with which Simon gave in to the request, and said so when they were left alone in the viewing room. A blind had dropped and they could see nothing of the cryogenic laboratory.

'No point, Bogie. When we make a noise, I want it to be for something important. Not just to talk to that boy. What'd you make of him?'

'Hesher.' The single word was loaded with contempt. Even in the enlightened atmosphere that existed on most of the worlds within the Federation, homosexuality was something that Eugene Bogart had never managed to come to terms with.

'I thought he looked like it,' muttered Simon. 'Odd really, that. I'd have expected a straight. Considering whom they're dealing with. You reckon Razan's a hesher?'

Bogie laughed. 'Nope. Friggin' creepy, but not a hesher. So we go back to our room?'

'Could be worse, Bogie. You've never seen this kind of luxury before. Make the most of it. And don't forget why we're here.'

'Right.' They walked together along the corridor, ignoring the patrolling guards. 'Simon? Why do you reckon that they wouldn't let us speak to that frozen kid?'

'I don't know, Bogie. Maybe cold feet!'

There was one nasty moment when they returned to their room. Somehow, Zeta's dog, the unpleasant Humphrey, had got in while they were out, and performed various anti-social acts on Bogie's bed and in three places on the rich carpet. When they tried to get it out it flew into a hysterical state and yapped and snapped at them, eyes almost bursting from its fat little head.

'Shall I snuff it, Simon?' asked Bogart, losing patience with trying to trap the brute.

'No. Give it a break.'

'Like its neck?' grinned Bogie, waving his colt at it.

At a ring, three attendants came running in, recoiling for a moment from the uncontrolled venom of the dog. But they finally managed to remove it, and also all the traces of its presence.

'I've seen some little bastards, but that friggin' bitch beats all.'

'It's not a bitch. Humphrey is all butch, and he's my only friend left in the world. If you'd touched him, I'd have had your eyes ripped out!'

The high-pitched voice from the doorway was Zeta Price, his hair now dyed purple and pink, with gown patterned to match. He had heard of the incident with Humphrey and had come running from the lounge to see what he could do.

Both Simon and Bogart were so taken aback by the outburst that they just stood there, looking at the angry little man, until he sniffed and stalked off on his high heels, to retrieve his precious from a sentry.

'Should have broken its neck. Maybe his too,' was Bogie's only comment.

Someone saved him the trouble.

During the night, when they all should have been sleeping

54

soundly, someone in Paradise managed to get to Humphrey. It was Zeta who found the little corpse when he got up, and promptly fainted, after giving a theatrical scream that brought everyone not doped up running to his room. Simon and Bogie were among the first there, both holding their colts. When they saw what had happened, they holstered them in their belts, withdrawing a little from the scene.

Price was injected by a medic with a massive dose of a trank, then carried off to the superbly equipped hospital. The body of the dog was removed, its head hanging limply on its broken neck, eyes suffused with blood, swollen tongue protruding from its mouth.

'You?'

Bogie stepped back in mock amazement. 'Me! Simon! How can you? After all we've been through.'

'Come on, Bogie. This is too important to frig around with things like killing dogs. Did you?'

They walked back to their room. 'No. No, I didn't. I wish I had, and I'm not crying over the snotty little bitch.'

'Butch.'

'Butch! I couldn't have got out without waking you, and you know it.'

'Yeah, that's true.' They slid the door behind them, and sat on their beds. 'I reckon that most everyone on Paradise hated Humphrey.'

'Or Price.'

'Yes.'

For a moment they sat in silence, then Rack climbed into bed, pulling the cover up to his chest. Lay down, and then suddenly sat up again.

'Wait a minute. That's a curious incident of that dog in the night.'

Bogie looked puzzled. 'But the dog itself didn't do anything.'

Simon grinned. '*That* was the curious incident!'

FOUR

AS ONE DOOR CLOSES, ANOTHER DOOR CLOSES

'Two days gone, and what the hell have we got to show for it? Bogie? Nothing. Frig-all! Not a whisper of the genetic code. Not a hint of murder. Just the easy life and five days to go to the big freeze.'

Bogart was dozing on his bed, a glass of amber liquor at his elbow. At Simon's bitter speech, he sat up, grinning across at him. 'Come on, Simon. Something'll come up. It always does. And you've got to admit this is the easiest mission any officer ever drew. The only danger is eating yourself to death or being sucked dry by one of those pleasure machines Razan's got in the sex rooms.'

The vibrating of Simon's bed ceased immediately he got up off it and walked over to Bogie. 'Listen, you walking accident! If we don't get that code back, then there aren't ever going to be any easy missions. Not ever again. If the wrong person's got it and uses it cleverly, then there probably won't ever be *any* kind of mission. You're getting lulled by this damned place. It's not really Paradise, Bogie. There's a snake around in this garden, as the Christians would say, and we've got just four and a half days to find him.'

'Or her?'

'Or her.'

The members of the party had all been enjoying the facilities of the station in their own different ways. And none of them seemed to have been disappointed. There was a feeling running through Paradise of ease and relaxation. There had been no more rows, except the obvious tension between the Girondes, and even Price was smiling at von Neumann and getting a grudging smile back. It was this lethargy that had obviously got to Bogie, and it was this that worried Simon.

Angelika Wellcome seemed to have got over her initial depression and spent much of her time in the main lounge, either watching some vid-books or just walking round her sonic sculptures, talking softly to them, enjoying their melodious responses.

Von Neumann and Rafael Strafford spent a lot of time in each other's company, talking quietly in rooms, and walking slowly round the perimeter of the station. The diplomat was clearly dying, although the pain-killers were keeping him mobile during his last few days. Strafford was the stronger of the two, occasionally supporting von Neumann.

Viki Laurel was constantly in the grip of drugs. Sometimes she slept, agonised, racking dreams torturing her, and at other times she walked the ship, nervously topped up, talking to anyone who'd listen and to nobody if there was nobody. Despite the tranks, she seemed to have aged ten years since she boarded the shuttle back on Crucis. A couple of times she looked as though she was going to talk to Simon. To reveal something of importance. It could so easily be some kind of guilt she wanted to unload to one of the only two men who were scheduled to come back from Paradise.

Rack kept close to Viki Laurel, waiting for the moment when she'd break down her own barriers and talk to him. He figured it couldn't be that long.

Zeta Price also spent a lot of time in sleep. The brutal death of his beloved pet had stricken him, and he was a sad, aged figure when he came again among them. His hair was bleached to its proper colour. His clothes were quiet, seeming to hang about him like a curtain on a drowned man. His brittle chatter was subdued. He spoke quietly to anyone who'd acknowledge him and seemed pathetically glad for the response.

On one occasion, he'd confided to Bogart that he only waited now for the days to drag by so that he could sleep and sleep. The idea of wakening again seemed of little interest.

The Girondes kept to themselves. Twice raised voices echoed round the ship from their quarters, and once Ruth appeared for a meal with make-up failing to hide the imprint of a fist on her face. Wallace was the only one on board who made a lot of use of the sex rooms, playing happily under the supervision of the medics on some of the climax simulators.

They only saw Razan at formal meals, which were not in any way compulsory, and which most of the guests opted out of anyway. The Exalted Leader of Paradise seemed happier now that things were running more smoothly his way and was positively expansive at one of the meals. At the dinner on the second day, he waxed lyrical on the limitless talents they had at their disposal in the mem-banks of the comps.

'There is no food that we cannot reproduce here, and no drink that will not please the palate of a guest. Some have tried to challenge us – it is in the nature of the rich and the powerful to do that – but we have never been beaten. Never. It is, I think, impossible.'

But his almost supernatural calm was displaced by Bogie, to the disgust of von Neumann and the great enjoyment of Simon Rack.

'That reminds me of an eater on, where was it, Simon? Was it Sturdal?'

Simon nodded. He spotted that this was going to be one of Bogart's stretched stories, and knew from experience that facts would come low in the narrator's priorities.

'Yes, it was. This eater was the biggest in the universe. Boasted it was the biggest in the galaxy. Claimed that there was no dish known to man that they couldn't supply within one hour. Anything. Promised a million credits to anyone who could prove them wrong and catch them out. They were nearly as confident as you are, Razan.'

Suspecting that he could end up as the butt of the tale, the thin man bowed his head slightly, eyes glittering in their hooded sockets.

'In comes this fellow. Sits down. Looks at the menu, which ran to several hundred pages. Puts it down. Calls over the waiter. Says: "If I order any food you can't supply within the hour, then you pay me a million credits?" Waiter looks at him pityingly. They get them all the time, and they never lose. "Yes sir," he says. "Right," says the man. "Bring me the foreskin of a khetam on toast.' Now the khetam is a rare sort of creature that lives on the frontier world of Zayin. Very rare. Waiter takes the order and goes off.'

The guests round the table were interested in spite of themselves. Simon had a vague feeling that he'd heard this one before, and sat back sipping at the fine light blue wine.

'Half an hour goes by, and the manager comes out. "Are you the gentleman who asked for the foreskin of a khetam on toast?" "Yes," he says. "I see," says the manager, going off back to the prep rooms. Another half hour goes by, and the manager comes out, looking very depressed. Puts down a note for a million credits. "Sorry, sir," he says, miserably, "there's your credits. You beat us. We've run out of bread." '

The third day opened in the same way as the others. Simon just prowled about the station, picking up things and putting them down again. Unable to settle, conscious of the way time was dribbling away. That the mist would soon rise and envelop the capsules and he and Bogie would be sent back to Crucis with a total blank failure to mark on their records. It had happened before, even though they had the highest mission success rate of any duo in the Galactic Security Organisation. But previous failures would pale into nothing by the side of this one.

Bogart got up late, selecting a lime-green robe from the wardrobe, tightening the belt and strapping his colt in place.

'Figure I might go and try one of those pleasure machines that Wallace Gironde spends all his time playing with. How 'bout you?'

Simon lay back on his own bed, scratching his chin. 'Usual. Probe away at people and see what I can dig up. Think I might go for Viki Laurel.'

'I'll do that, if you like. Always worshipped that little doll. You talk to Miss Wellcome.'

Simon made a very rude gesture that they had picked up in the Omicron Galaxy. It involved tongue and both thumbs, and would have meant death if anyone had seen it on its home planet. All the response he got from Bogie was a cheerful and more traditional gesture that only involved one finger of one hand, followed by a rude noise.

While Bogie went his way to the private pleasure rooms, Simon walked slowly to the lounge, looking for Viki Laurel. The only one there was von Neumann, eyes closed, listening to the flow and beauty of the sculptures. They reacted slightly to Simon's arrival by changing pitch, and the politician opened his eyes.

He was still the most resistant to the presence of the two officers on Paradise, and barely acknowledged Simon's arrival.

'Good day, Rack.'

'Sir. Would you have been Miss Laurel around at all this morning?'

'No. If I had I doubt I'd tell you. Now go away and leave me alone. Your presence here is offensive to me and is upsetting the tones of the sculptures.'

Simon never was all that patient with authority, and he stood directly in front of the grey-haired man, raising his voice. The sculptures whined in protest, then all sank into a sullen silence.

'I expect rudeness from mindless heshers like Price, or arrogant cretins like Gironde. But I reckon I ought to get a little more from one of the greatest diplomats in the history of the Federation! If it hadn't been for GalSec guards, you'd have been killed a dozen times.'

Mouth working with anger, von Neumann stood up, his pain forgotten, drowned in rage. 'You overstep your . . .'

'Don't give me that dreck. I checked up. Four GalSec officers gave their lives in stopping attempts on your life. Four men dead just to keep you alive. I hope their widows think it was worth it.'

He spun on his heel and stalked away, finding it hard to keep his hands from shaking. Just as he reached the doorway, von Neumann shouted after him. 'One more try like that, Rack, and I'll have you broken so small you won't need to open doors any more. You'll be able to crawl out under them!'

Just coming into the lounge was Rafael Strafford, and he touched Rack on the shoulder. 'Peace, brother. Karl was once, as you say, a great man. Pain has torn him apart, until he can no longer remember what he was. Only that his sole chance of becoming it again lies in those capsules in four days' time. Anything, *anything* that seems a threat will get trodden on. I would keep away from him, Simon. He still does have the power to ruin you.'

The quiet words worked with Simon. He took three deep breaths and smiled at the black man's face. 'Thanks, Rafael. I'm grateful. And I'll bear it in mind.'

Before he went to sit down by the shaking figure of von Neumann, Strafford gave Simon another word of advice. 'If you're looking for that poor child, Viki Laurel, she spends a lot of time in the relaxer pool. Try there.'

She was there.

There were two adjoining pools, one for men and one for women. Simon walked softly into the right-hand one, past the blank-faced sentry. The wall between the pools was thin, and he could hear the fluting voice of the vid-star, singing quietly away to herself. He was pleased to hear that she sounded as though she was in the happy land between uppers and downers. Pitching his voice low, he called through to her. The singing stopped, and he heard her splashing through the water to be nearer to the wall.

'Simon?'

'Yes. Can I speak to you for a bit? I'm feeling lonely and I thought . . .'

It was a lie. Lonely wasn't what he felt, but it struck the chord he hoped with the disturbed girl. 'There's a door at the far end. Wait a minute and I'll unlock it from my side. You can come through and nobody'll know. Lock the outer door first so we aren't interrupted.'

That was an invitation he couldn't refuse, and he slipped the catch on the outer door and stepped quickly round the still water, until he was in the ladies' side. Viki had clambered out to meet him, and sat on the side, dabbling her toes elegantly in the scented, steaming water. A robe was hung over her white shoulders, pulled carelessly round her breasts, revealing the valley but concealing the peaks.

'Sit down by me, Simon, and talk to me of nice things. Make me happy for a while. I've wanted you too for . . . well, since we got to Paradise.'

Prompted by Viki, he stripped off his robe, dropping it on the warm marble, making sure from force of habit that the butt of his colt lay conveniently near his hand. While he undressed, Viki had slipped from her robe, and eased down into the water, her pale body vanishing into a blur of movement. Unselfconscious himself, Simon was struck by her casual approach to her own body, and to his. After one long, appraising look she virtually ignored him as he entered the pool beside her.

Only the most luxurious stations had this sort of pool, and Simon closed his mind to the way it had been recycled from bodily wastes. It felt good to immerse himself in the scented warmth, rolling over and over, dipping his head under the surface, blinking at the steamy figure of Viki Laurel. As with his encounter with Ruth Gironde, Simon found it hard to come to terms with the reality of the situation. Here he was, bathing nude with *Viki Laurel. The* Viki Laurel, whose body had lent a touch of class to the top grossers among vids in the last five years. Bathing with her, like some leading man. But with one difference. There was no crew. No cameras. No eyes to see. The thought hit him hard, and he found that he was developing an embarrassing erection.

Viki surfaced at the end of the pool, hanging on to the silver rail, hair streaming over her shoulders in a white torrent. Simon was unable to resist the temptation to peek, seeing that she really was a natural blonde. All the way through. Face cleaned of all make-up, she looked very young and vulnerable. Grinning at him cheekily, she beckoned him over with a crooked finger. He dived in and swam easily across, resting one hand on the rail by her arm.

'Simon. I have to talk to you. Before I go . . . off to be chilled . . . there's something I have to tell, and you're the only one I can trust.'

Gently, Simon kissed her on the flawless neck, muttering a silent prayer to his guardian angel. It looked as though it was going to be a good one after all.

The door of the pleasure room was locked. The four-wall display was, at the moment, bathed in a pink glow, ready for the subject to process any scenes he wanted on them from the vast micro-library of Paradise. Any place, any time, any people. Doing anything.

Bogart had already decided what he wanted to watch while the machine did its stuff for him. The only thing that put him off a bit was the colour of the pleasure machine, which was bright green. Still, once one had shut oneself firmly inside and connected the . . . connections to whatever parts of the body, the colour wouldn't matter a bit.

That was what he heard, anyway.

Naked, the tufts of hair on his chest slicked down by the sweat of anticipation, Bogie stepped inside, hands working away as he joined the tubes and probes to himself, following the detailed instructions. He'd have preferred proper girls, but that was one thing that Paradise didn't have. Razan had explained that the sexual drives were too basic and too complex for them to risk any possibility of involvement with real ladies. Or men, come to that. And the balance of harmony on the station was such a fine one that anything could jar it out of its pattern of light and beauty.

So, the machine was the thing. Bogie had heard of them, but he'd never actually seen one. He knew he'd regret it all his life if he didn't seize the opportunity now, while he had the chance. Smiling to himself, at the thought of what some of his mates off the starships would say if they could see him now, all trussed up like a joint of meat ready for the roaster. He pressed the start button, and the machine began to hum and vibrate. Moving pictures began to appear on the walls, watched eagerly by Bogie.

As things began to happen, he closed his eyes and gave himself over to the pleasure. Lights flickered on the master control board on the other side of the room, with its red over-rule button, for giving of pleasure to any degree. Unnoticed by the euphoric Bogie, the catch on the main door began to slide back.

Very slowly.

It wasn't what he wanted.

'Wait a minute, Viki. You mean that your career is so frigging vital that you're risking your life for it?'

The balance was going fast. While she caressed him absently, she whispered her story. Simon was stunned. And shaken by it. Gradually, her words had come faster, and she had twice broken down crying, unable to carry on. But finally the whole messy business had come out.

In a nutshell, the career of Viki Laurel stood at the crossroads. Her last two vids hadn't been flops. Not by a million miles. But they hadn't grossed like they should have done. The moguls who controlled the business had suspected that she was about to take the plunge downwards. But a clever adman at the front office had come up with a great idea that everyone liked.

Viki would die. The story of leukaemia was put about, then denied, then finally admitted. The trip to Paradise was a phony. She wasn't ill, and she was going in for only the minimum of six months. All the time she'd be away, the publicity wagon would try and keep rolling, and her vids would be shown all over the galaxy.

'And then you come back and you're miraculously better. All trace of illness gone?'

'Right, lover. I've already taped the scene in the capsule with my famous last words. It'll go great. Not a dry eye in the universe. Then I come back even bigger than ever.'

As she told him the whole sick plot, Viki had slowly changed the slant. When she began, when she was fairly normal, it had been the truth. That her career was slumping and this was a desperate gambit to save it. Then it altered. It became that her career was still stupendous, and that this was merely a minor way of boosting it. That her fans would appreciate her *even* more after a few months away.

As the tale changed, so she became more and more worried about having vomited it up to a stranger. Her hands had roamed more insistently, taking his hands, and tugging at him to make him do things to her. Although he'd have done anything for her when he got in the water, the truth had changed his desire, and it was all he could do not to get out and leave. But the vid-star was in such a state now that if he left he

65

guessed that she would freak out over the top.

There was only one way that she could work off her guilt, and that was make love to him. Finally, since it was inevitable, Simon lay back in the warm water and began to enjoy it. Hot lips nibbled at him, sucking and teasing his flesh. Viki's long fingers probed at him, doing things he'd only ever read about in the pornoes, rousing him and bringing him to the brink of climax, then skilfully holding him back.

In return, he did what he could, but it was essentially a one-woman passion play, and he was just a mute instrument for her to work on. It made a change, and he began to enter more into the spirit of things. The water splashed and waves broke over them, making them both gasp for breath. Grinding together, they at last neared a stunning climax.

Bogie was well on the way towards a stunning climax. The machine took some getting used to, but the controls were simple to master. It all boiled down to whether you wanted it fast or slow. Bogie had always wanted it slow. Things seemed to be moving on nicely, despite the strange fact that the machine was going just that bit faster than he'd set it. But it was close. Getting closer.

He closed his eyes and let the machine have its way with him. It really wasn't bad.

It really hadn't been bad. The orgasm also seemed to have helped Viki and she was relaxing once again in the water when Simon dressed quietly and slipped back into the men's side, unlocking the door and walking out past the guard into the corridor.

Apart from the obvious physical benefit, he hadn't learned much. That was two of the three ladies gone and one to go. Although Angelika Wellcome seemed a nice enough old lady, Simon hoped that it wouldn't be necessary for him to . . . Not with her.

66

He knew where Bogie would be, and decided to go to the lounge and sit around there. Maybe the very sight of him would be enough to make the guilty member of the party just up and hand over the code.

Maybe.

Simon wished that something would happen. And fast.

Bogart wished that someone would come along, and fast.

The machine was running on, long after he'd pressed the automatic cut-out. Long after it had milked him dry. The door was jammed and he couldn't move, nor did he dare to try and rip off the sucking and tugging attachments. They were too firmly linked to him.

He'd shouted for a bit, before realising that the doors were sound-proofed to shut out the screams of pleasure that the machine was supposed to give. His first thought had been it was a mechanical fault, but that didn't seem likely. Not on a place as well run as Paradise. So? So someone had fixed it. Someone was out to murder him.

The pressures went on. He could feel liquid trickling slowly down the inside of both thighs. It could have been sweat. He prayed it was. The soreness was agonising, making him feel as though his genitals had been sand-blasted and then caught in a cross between a vacuum pump and a vice.

He'd soon black out from the pain. Bogie knew his body well enough, and knew the limitations it could put up with. Once he passed out, the strain on his private parts would become intolerable. There would be ripping and tearing of all that he held dear, then massive haemorrhaging.

Time was running out.

Von Neumann and Strafford were still there in the lounge when Simon walked in, talking with their heads close together. The diplomat looked up, and broke off the conversation.

'Commander Rack, if you are going to be in this room, then

I and my companion will leave it. I have had a surfeit of people like you in my life, and I repeat my promise. If you get in my way once more, I will use all my influence to have you removed.'

Simon paused, about to sit down, and walked instead to the door. 'I'm going. Nice talking to you.' If Bogart wasn't finished, then he'd go back to his room.

Bogie was nearly finished.

Like some infernal parody of his predicament, the lively figures on the walls still capered and coupled, but he was long past appreciating them. His head was dropping, and blood ran down his chin from where he'd bitten his lips trying not to lose consciousness. Somewhere at the corner of his mind he seemed to see a red light blinking on and off.

'Belted and ready,' he muttered, wondering what was holding up the blast-off. He could just catch Simon's voice, calling his name, and he tried to shut it out, ready to concentrate on the crushing force of lifting off in the two-seater scouts. But the voice continued.

'Aaaaaaaaaahhhhh!!!!!' Summoning up all of his fading strength, Bogie screamed out for help, realising at last where he was and what was happening.

Outside, Simon pushed the sentry out of the way. 'Unlock it. Fast!'

'No. No door is to be ...'

Simon hit him a clubbing blow with the heel of his hand, slamming the man's jaws shut with a sickening splinter of broken bone and teeth. The guard slumped unconscious at his feet, an alarm button going automatically. Simon didn't hesitate, whipping out the blaster and setting it at maximum, pointing it at the centre of the door and firing it in three short bursts.

The lock charred and fell out, and he ran in, taking in what was happening in a second, running to the wall panel and switching over the master cut-out.

After that, it was easy. The bright green doors opened and he quickly and gently pulled off the dormant tubes and suckers, now limp and silent. He grimaced at the blood streaking Bogie's thighs and groin. Tenderly, he carried his partner to a couch, wiping the worst of the streaking from him with a strip torn from his robe. He ignored a crowd gathering in the doorway watching him. Ignored Razan who had come in, a needle gun in his claws, then stepped back when he saw what was happening.

It wasn't as bad as he'd feared. Most of the tissue damage was superficial, caused by the friction burns as the machine ran on and on. While he worked, Bogie's eyes fluttered open, and he groaned.

'Bogie? See who did it?' That was the most important question. Others could come later.

'No. No.'

Razan stepped forwards again, the gun now stowed away under his black robes. 'My dear Brothers. How can this dreadful thing have happened? We make the most careful checks, and I can . . .'

'Stow it, Razan. Get him to the sick-bay. He's got the constitution of a sludge tanker, but . . .'

Von Neumann appeared in the doorway, pushing through the line of sentries. Seeing what had happened to Bogie, he sniffed. 'That will teach him to poke his nose into the affairs of others.'

Simon had the choice of hitting him or not. He chose not. 'It wasn't his nose, and why don't you sod off to your deathbed.'

From the look on the diplomat's face, he wondered if maybe it wouldn't have been better to have hit him. Bogart was trying to sit up, sweat pouring off him.

'Wait there, Bogie. How do you feel?'

The eyes crinkled, and a ghost of a grin crossed his partner's lips. 'You really want to know? I feel absolutely fucked!'

FIVE

SOMEBODY UP THERE DOESN'T . . .

Three days to go.

Whatever else was true about Paradise, their medical care was the best that Simon Rack had ever come across. Their facilities were even better than those at the headquarters of GalSec. Only once had Simon been severely enough injured to merit transport to Base, but he remembered it well. The memory made him rub at the wrist. Good though they'd been, the damage had been so radical that he'd been told it would always be a potential weakness. He'd got through all the medicals without trouble, but they'd been right. He knew it. He was the only one who knew it.

Bogie was back on his feet by that morning, heavily strapped up under his robe, walking with some difficulty, though mobility increased during the day. Doped up, he'd been told to rest, but that wasn't his way, and he kept up and moving, making painful circuit after circuit of the perimeter corridor, ignoring the blazing needles of starlight.

Razan had been profuse with his apologies, offering all manner of inducement to keep the matter quiet. All of which had been turned down by Bogie, at Simon's pressing instigation.

'Gives us a bit of a hold over him. Knowing that we might go back to Crucis and blow it all out about how you were nearly killed there. Could cut their trade.'

So the day passed quietly. Until just before the evening meal was being served. Wallace Gironde was being helped towards the marble table by his wife, when he stumbled and nearly fell. Ruth tried to help him, but he slipped, falling heavily, pulling her down on top of him. She rolled over, holding him by the arm, offering assistance.

Simon and Bogie also moved in to help, but stopped, repelled by the bitter hatred and anger on the multi-millionaire's face. He swung open-handed at Ruth, hitting her just above the eye, blood gushing from the cut. She made no move to avoid a second blow. Wallace wore several chunky rings on his gnarled fingers, and they ripped a strip of bloody flesh from his wife's white face. He was poised for another punch when Simon moved in, lifting him as effortlessly as he would a baby, setting him shakily on his feet. Stepping between him and his wife.

'Do that just one more time, and I'll break your damned neck like a rotten stick.'

Spittle sprayed out with the venom of the old man's rage. 'You fucking young bastard! ! I'll have you killed for this. I can. I'll have you skinned and use you for a shithouse cleaner. I have a man who'll take out every bone from your body and leave you alive. Like a human jelly-fish. You stand away and let me teach this fucking slut a lesson! !'

It was somehow appalling to hear the threats and foul language from a man old enough to be Simon's great-grand-father. The words were dreadful, and it seemed to Simon that they might just have a basis in reality. He made a mental note to have Gironde's friends and associates checked out when they got back to Crucis. Whatever faults the Federation had, it would rarely try and evade its responsibilities on the grounds of position or power. Rarely, but sometimes.

Ruth stood there, face white as the gown she wore, blood from the two cuts trickling unchecked down her neck, staining the robe. She still made no attempt to move away from the blind fury of her husband.

Rack looked at Wallace Gironde, seeing him clearly as a man who had lived far too long. Who had once learned that

71

money could buy you everything and everybody, and had never forgotten it.

'I pity you, Gironde. There's no way you can hurt me, or any man here, so you take out your spite and your senile anger on that woman.'

'Leave him,' said Ruth suddenly. 'You'll only make him worse when he's like this. He's capable of anything. Please.'

Once again, Gironde's anger focused on his wife. His eyes glittered like a poisonous reptile, and the muscles of his jaw stood out with the strain of fury. Veins throbbed in his forehead, and a thread of saliva edged greasily across his furrowed chin.

'Remember, Ruth. What I am and what we know. One word more from you and it will happen. A message and he dies. You know this. You'll pay me a high price for what has happened here now. Come. We will not eat. I want you alone.'

Bogart watched with contempt. 'You pitiful old fool. If I thought it would help, I'd throw you out of that vaporiser chute myself. Trouble is, it'd contaminate space with your rotting remains.'

There was the soft sound of applause from behind them, where Rafael Strafford had come in unnoticed and seen the little drama. 'Hear, hear, Eugene. Hear, hear.'

Baited on all sides, Wallace turned his head on his thin neck like a trapped rat, actually grinding his teeth in his anger. 'I'll . . . I'll have you all . . . you . . . I'll see you all in . . . in . . .'

'Hell,' said Bogie quietly as the old man's hands went to his throat, and he collapsed on the floor, fingers clenching, face turning blue.

'Better get him help, Mrs Gironde,' said Simon, thinking of what she'd told him would happen once Gironde actually died.

But she didn't seem to hear him, standing quite still, looking down at her husband grovelling in agony at her feet, one hand actually holding her ankle, mouth working as he tried to speak.

An expression of disgust crossed her white face, and she pulled away from him, walking slowly across the eating-room and vanishing in the direction of her suite.

The three men stood looking at Gironde as he wriggled, his movements growing slower and feebler. Then, they looked at each other. Strafford spoke: 'Well, gentlemen. I fear I've just forgotten something in my room. I will now go and get it. Returning in about ten minutes. I trust that will be long enough.'

'No. For reasons we can't tell you, he mustn't die. It matters to other people.'

'When he smiled, the mob laughed. When he cried, the little children died in the streets.' Stafford looked down at Gironde. 'Something like that. Epitaph for a tyrant. Very well, if you must save that object, I suggest you do it quickly. I think he has little time left.'

While Simon called assistance, Bogie stood looking down at the still figure. 'Doesn't seem very big now, does he? It's a waste of time keeping him alive for another three days, just to freeze him and let him go on with his evil for thousands of years more. Why freeze him? Why not just leave him out in the cold?'

Gironde was put once again in the intensive care section of the medical wing of Paradise. Razan reported to them over a subdued evening meal that his chances of surviving longer than a week were more or less nil.

'But as our brother is to go on that great journey in just seventy-two hours, our experts think that he will live that long, although in a comatose state.'

'Like carrying a man out on a stretcher to be shot,' commented Bogart through a mouthful of a superb sorbet.

'Hardly, Brother Bogart. Hardly,' replied the Exalted Leader, looking pained.

'Ruth? Mrs Gironde?'

'Aah, Brother Simon, I see you are concerned more for the lady than for her husband.'

Strafford interrupted Razan. 'If you'd been there like I was, you wouldn't give a flying crap for that little bastard. And you would care for his poor wife. Right?'

'Of course, Brother Rafael. She is being tended, and has been sedated and is resting quietly. Those cuts on her face have also been tended.'

'I'm glad. Now, it's late, and I'm going for a last walk before I turn in. See you back at the room, Bogie.'

He walked out of the lounge, thinking about Ruth Gironde and the sacrifice she was about to make for a man she loved. Or for a man she hated. It all depended on which way you looked at it. Just for the moment, Simon found the clinging richness of the station overpowering him, and he wished he could be away into deep space again with Bogie on some nice simple mission. Breaking a few heads would be good right now, he thought.

There was something about Paradise that Simon found hard to take. There was the overwhelming richness and decay. A mix of drugs and opulence. 'Amphetamines and pearls,' he whispered to himself, not even sure where the line came from, but just liking it.

Three days to go, and then the remaining men and women would be plunged into the mists of forgetfulness. Except that all the evidence was that they wouldn't forget. One day, some time, one of them would wake up with a secret that could provide them with the key to unlock all the power in the galaxy.

He leaned against the rail, padded with a dark burgundy velvet, and stared out over the stars through one of the observation panels, brilliant and clear despite the slight distortion of the meteorite deflector shield. Who could it be? They were all still possibles. And what about Razan? Both he and Bogie

74

had caught him several times standing wrapt in thought as though he were waiting for some kind of instructions. If he wasn't in charge of Paradise, then who was? Whoever had come up with the whole idea had to be a real genius.

Floyd Thursby? Whoever was he? Simon shook his head and turned abruptly to walk back to try and talk some plan up with Bogie. The bolt from the needle gun plucked at the edge of his robe like an angry creditor, singeing a hole clean through it.

If he'd stayed where he was, the bolt would have hit him round about the base of the skull and killed him. At that moment, the lights all went out and there was the briefest fraction of slowing down. Simon felt his weight slip away as gravity dropped, then emergency motors cut in again and the feeling vanished. But it still stayed dark.

Another crack from the hidden assassin, and the tickle of air against his cheek that told him the gun either had a heat seeker or a night-scope fitted. It wasn't a good thing to be shot at with either. Particularly in darkness.

Their combat instructor in his early days in GalSec had been full of wise advice. Simon might have skipped some of the talks on etiquette and protocol, but never the ones on how to kill and how to save yourself from being killed.

The furniture in the corridor was sparse, but there was, fortunately, a heavy chair, made of chromed steel, set against the inner wall of the circular station. Colt firing off a random shot in the blackness, Simon dived behind it, relieved to hear and feel the vicious impact of another needle bolt against the seat.

The instructor had said: 'If your man's got all the cards, make him show his hand. Any way you can.'

Simon crouched silent, listening. There was the sound of heavy breathing from near the door, and voices farther away, shouting for light. The pitch of the breathing altered slightly, as though it was a very fat man shuffling along on his hands and knees. On an impulse, Rack snapped off a bolt at low level, where he thought the noise had come from. There was a muffled yelp of pain, and the sound of something being knocked over.

There was the slit of a light showing under a door behind his assailant, and he caught a glimpse of something moving across it. At the same time he heard Bogie's voice, calling out his name.

If he shouted back, then the man might shoot at the sound and kill him. If he didn't, the door would swing open and Bogie would stand there blinking, a perfect silhouette.

'Needle gun!! Behind door!!' he shouted, at the same time flinging himself backwards.

The shot was high, as he'd hoped, setting fire to a small tapestry above his head, the flames flickering and guttering. A draught nibbled at the fire, and then there was silence. Beyond the door, Bogie was also quiet, waiting for some word from Simon to clue him in.

Silence.

He counted to a hundred, waiting for the man to breathe. Holding his own breath.

Nothing.

Cautiously, he risked a shot in the direction that he'd last seen the man. The draught had stopped, like a door had been shut silently somewhere off the corridor.

'Bogie!! Push the door open, and watch yourself. I think he's gone, and he didn't go past me.'

The main door from the lounge and eater opened slowly, and an edge of white light flooded in, showing Simon that he'd been right. The corridor was empty.

It took them only about a minute to find out where the would-be killer had fled. There was another door, its edges blending into the geometric pattern of the wall blocks. There was no handle, and it resisted any attempt to force it. While

Simon and Bogart thrust and pushed at it, Razan appeared, out of breath, and looking more upset than at any time since they'd arrived in Paradise.

'Brothers!! Brothers!' he cried. 'That door is to remain closed. It goes to a most secret place.' Yet again he paused, then went on, 'It hides the secrets of the cryogenic process and must not be breached. Remember our agreement.'

Simon still held his colt, the barrel warm. Reaching up high, he laid that barrel gently against the cheek of the Exalted Leader. 'Feel that, Brother Abraham. That door doesn't just hide a secret. It hides a damned killer. A man who's already killed at least once and is still trying to kill. Bogie here was nearly wasted in that machine, and I nearly got it in this corridor. Someone with a needle gun, like all of your guards. A big man who breathes heavy. Now who do you suppose that could be, Razan? Eh? Maybe the elusive Mister Thursby? Talk to me, Razan. Murder of a Federation officer in the execution of his duty could get this base closed down in no time flat. Come on.'

Razan seemed confused, his eyes glittering helplessly, wringing his hands. His hair was dishevelled, hanging loose over his ears. He looked this way and that as though he were seeking inspiration.

'Please. Commander. Don't call in your reinforcements. Please. I'm begging you. The people here will be frozen in another two days. Wait till then.'

Razan was obviously rattled, using a word like 'frozen' instead of 'gone before' or 'sleeping' or 'embarking upon the timeless journey to immortality'. For the first time, Simon began to think that things were beginning to move a little bit his way.

He ignored the plea. 'What happened to the power source? Seems to me this operation is winding down, Razan. Why don't I just speed it up for you?'

77

He recognised the voice, trembling on the edge of utter anger. Von Neumann was about to throw his considerable weight into things again.

'Commander, I have told you until I am tired. Apart from the sad death of Doctor Bulman, which you seem to have done nothing to solve, there is no reason to suppose that anything is wrong here. Your assistant bungles the setting on the machine and you attack a guard and nearly get shot as the penalty for your stupidity. Where is your killer? Gone, you say. I say that it is time that you were gone, Commander, I propose now communicating with certain friends that I still have back on Crucis. I give you my word that you and your bungling comrade will be off this station before the day is out.'

'Very well. I'm sorry about this, but I have no choice at all. Karl von Neumann, I'm arresting you on a charge of interfering with justice under Section Eight of Federation Law. When the shuttle comes in two days' time, I will take you with me back to Crucis for trial. That may take several weeks. Until we go back, you're free to move around Paradise as much as you want.'

Simon turned his back on the diplomat, ready to go to his own room. At that moment, all the lighting cut back in again. Out of the corner of his eye he saw Bogie staring at him, his face a conflicting mix of concern and delight.

'Wait.' The voice was frayed, uncertain. 'Commander Rack. I suggest you cannot do . . .'

He spun round, hand on his colt, face set in a grim smile. 'I am tired, von Neumann, of being told by you what I can and what I can't do. I am an officer of the Galactic Security Service and there is very little that I can't do if I really apply my mind to it.'

'But afterwards?' The aggression was gone, replaced by a vaguely querulous note.

'Afterwards, I may get it in the neck if I'm wrong. In this case I know I'm right. An eminent man murdered. Vital information stolen. Attempts to kill my colleague and me.'

'And Humphrey,' put in Zeta Price, who had at last appeared among them.

'It's too much, and *you* have done nothing but threaten me and hinder my attempts to solve the case. Now, you've gone too far and I've arrested you. Don't worry, von Neumann. You'll get your chance to talk in court. Back on Crucis.'

'No. No . . . You don't . . . If I come back, then . . .'

'Then you'll die. Is that it? Too late to think on that, von Neumann. I take you back. Unless . . .' The word hung in the scented air, waiting for someone to pick it up. Simon looked round the room, waiting.

It was von Neumann. 'Commander.' The effort it was taking him was obvious. 'Perhaps if we were to try again, then I think things might be different.'

That was too easy for him. That wasn't how Simon wanted it. 'There's one way to make it different. You keep your damned mouth closed when I'm around! And no more of your empty threats. Is that clear? My threats aren't empty. The worst you can do to me is put my career back. I'm about the best there is at what I do, and I'm way down in promotion. Know why? Because, von Neumann, some of us don't want promotion and power. We just want to get along. It's people like me that you can't touch. But I can touch you. I can kill you. All very legal. What about that?'

The diplomat's voice was pitched so low that they could hardly hear it. 'Commander. I apologise. It's . . . very important to me that I be processed in two days. I have given my life for humanity, and I will not . . . I cannot . . . lose it all now. I must have that chance.'

'Right. What I said applies to everyone here. Including you, Razan. Any more obstruction and I close the station down and send for ships back to Crucis for help. One more piece of hindrance and you all come back.'

Standing to his full height, the hair now brushed back in

place, Abraham Razan seemed to have regained his poise and self-confidence. 'I am grateful that you have seen the revelation of the road to charity. We are all grateful to you.'

White coat partly unbuttoned, one of the guards came silently in and motioned for the Exalted Leader to go to him. Razan bowed his head and listened, his face betraying not the least sign of emotion. Then he waved the man away and rejoined the circle of men and women.

'In some ways, the situation has taken over events and hopes. You, my dear Brother Karl, could not harm Commander Rack, even if you now wished to do so. And you, Simon, could not call any reinforcements.'

'Why not?'

It was hard to see if Razan was smiling or not. His voice was unchanged, pitched low, harmonious and beautiful. 'I fear that we are cut off by the accident to our main controls. All the communications are useless. We are cut off until the next shuttle comes.' He stared intently at Rack. 'And that means after everyone has taken their long sleep.'

Back in their room again after the meal, Bogie kicked a pair of boots across the thick carpet. 'That means we've lost all our aces.'

Simon looked up at him and smiled. 'May be wrong, Bogie, but I've just thought who our joker may be. And that'll answer an awful lot of questions. All this freezing'll make sense.'

'Tell us.'

'Later. When I'm sure. I don't want to be the one to catch a cold!'

SIX

THE FRONT GOES BACK
AND THE BACK GOES FRONT

The time for the freezing was set for the middle of the afternoon on the next day. The seventh day. The next shuttle was
due to arrive just before that time, but the system of the
station meant that there would be absolutely no mingling at all
with the guests in the new party. Just as there had been none
with the previous group.

The night had passed well enough. Everyone seemed to be
approaching the end of their current lives with great calm.
Both Zeta Price and Viki Laurel were almost unrecognisable
from the screaming puppets they'd been when they left the
Crucis port. Strafford didn't seem to have changed at all,
remaining grave and yet immensely good-humoured. Wallace
Gironde was slowly losing his hold on life in an oxygen tent in
the medical section. Ruth had been warned that it might be
necessary for him to be frozen prematurely, but that this
would be done privately and with nobody else present. She
kept to her room, and had all her food sent to her.

Von Neumann maintained an uneasy peace with Simon,
being frostily polite, although it was clear that he was endur-
ing pain that almost crippled him.

The only one who seemed to be finding the waiting hard
was the lady sculptor, Angelika Wellcome. She was drinking
heavily, refusing all of the less harmful drugs that were offered
to her. Even turning down hashish, claiming that she preferred the taste of liquor. Twice she had become maudlin and

drunk at a meal, and once had been found in the main lounge in the middle of the night talking incoherently to the sonic sculptures she had created.

Razan was once more totally in control as he tried to help the party through the last forty-eight hours of waiting. Simon and Bogart made no further attempt to question anyone, contenting themselves with making careful efforts to find a way into the rear part of the station, but the guards were always there, and they were kept back.

It had been agreed that the afternoon should be given over to meditation. Razan announced it to the group after the morning meal. Before they split up to go wherever they wished, he held up his hand, the long robes trailing from his skinny wrists, the gold bracelets sparkling in the overhead lighting.

'Brothers and Sisters, I fear that I have tidings that will bring unhappiness to all.'

'You've run out of ice,' joked Bogie, still carrying on with his self-appointed task of puncturing the bubble of Razan's self-importance.

'That's in bad taste, young man,' snapped Miss Wellcome, trying to conceal an unladylike belch.

The Exalted Leader carried on as he always tried to as though there had been no interruption at all. 'Mrs Gironde has been informed and has asked that you should also be told. Her husband approached a critical point in the late hours of the night and our medical experts agreed that normal bodily functions could fail before it was time for him to enter the happy state beyond life.'

A loud sniff from Bogart.

Razan went on. 'So we have brought forward the process by one day, and Wallace Gironde already sleeps the sleep wherein there is no pain. Which goes on and yet shall cease. The sleep from which the only awakening is a happy one.'

'You've frozen him?'

'If you wish to put it like that, Brother Bogart, then, yes, we have frozen him. For those of you who wish to see him before he is placed in the capsule container, Sister Ruth has asked that her husband be left in the freezing room for one hour from now so that you may pay any last respects.'

Although it would be fair to say that Wallace Gironde would have featured near the bottom of anyone's popularity poll, it was something different to do. Beautiful and idyllic though Paradise was, it had limitations, and boredom was just beginning to be felt. Whoever ran Floyd Thursby Enterprises was shrewd enough to know that seven days was just long enough for everyone to calm down from their tensions and worries and not quite long enough for them to get too bored with the whole thing.

The casket was laid out in the ante-room of the Gironde suite, ready to be rolled away to the stacking and filing quarters they'd all seen vids and threedees of in the brochures. The top was sealed, but they saw that a clear panel was left in the lid, something that the mist and frost had obscured in the laboratories. They each filed past and looked down at the sleeping remains of Wallace Gironde. His hair combed, clothes straightened, and face touched up with the cosmeticist's skill, though they had refrained from the usual trick of putting a smile on the face of the body. His name and age and date were neatly stencilled on the case with the number of a file which would carry the details of resuscitation.

There was a chill to the casket and they could see that there was a faint mist inside, frosting the tips of the eyebrows and dusting the hair with silver. Tubes and cables connected all the life-support systems to the body, vanishing into a small portable cabinet. The tiny brother, they were told by Razan, of the massive complex behind the scenes.

Bogart took Simon on one side after he'd peered down at Gironde. 'Are you sure he's alive, Simon? I'd swear that was a dead one.'

'I thought that, Bogie, but I've never seen a freezer before.

I suppose they probably look alike. Anyway, those life-support readers are all positive.'

The readers were a panel of indicators showing that life was not extinct, although heart and all motor functions had ceased. A small red light glowed in a slow pattern, and an electronic blip moved monotonously and regularly from one side of a dial to the other.

'All I can say is, that Sleeping Beauty he ain't, Simon.'

Despite the premature disappearance of her husband, Ruth Gironde still didn't appear. Although there seemed to be no reason why she should still go through with the cryogenic treatment, both Simon and Bogie knew she had no real choice. His black fingers reached out from beyond the vale of sleep to draw her after him.

Bogart had decided to take advantage of the suggestion of a meditation period, though for him that simply meant an extra chance to get some more sleep. He excused it on the grounds that he'd need to be at his sharpest ready for the next day, but Simon had once seen him go for nearly five days without any sleep and still function amazingly well. It was just that he liked sleeping.

Before he dropped off, he mentioned something that he'd seen when he left the viewing of the Gironde human icicle earlier than the others.

'I saw the hesher again. What's his name? Kornelis. Unless it was someone done up like him.'

'Where?'

Bogart yawned. 'In the corridor, where someone had a go at you. Wearing a sort of loincloth thing in gold, and his hair speckled with that glitter powder. Proves what I said about him. Friggin' hesher! Probably Floyd Thursby's little lover whom he keeps stashed away in that back part of the station. When he saw me he bolted like a scared raggin. By the time I got there he'd vanished. Could have gone on the way round the perimeter walk, but I reckon he went through that so-secret door in the bulkhead. Left behind a stink of cheap perfume.'

'I see. A strange boy who looks like a hesher.'

'Is a hesher!'

'All right. *Is* a hesher, then. Something really is odd about Paradise. The more I see of Razan, the more I'm sure that he doesn't run it. He's a front. Last night, when there was that shot at me, and I hit whoever it was, he took his time appearing and he was hellishly flustered. Didn't seem to know what to say. As though his control had gone away and left him all exposed. The bits are all falling in together, Bogie. I just hope we can get it together in time for the big freeze tomorrow afternoon. Otherwise we'll have a lump of mystery and six frozen suspects.'

Bogie dropped back on his pillow, closing his eyes. The bed immediately rocked him slowly, making him yawn again. Simon walked around, wondering about the enigmas that the bland, rich face of Paradise held concealed from him.

'I'm going for a walk. See if I can find a way past the sentries for a change. See you.' There was no reply. 'Bogie!'

'Oh, what?'

'Forget it. Go back to sleep.'

'No. I was just resting with my eyes closed. That's all. What did you say?'

'Just that I'm going for a walk and that I may be some time. See you.'

Dropping off, Bogie made the oldest of space jokes, maybe even dating back before the neutronic wars. But a joke that never seemed to pall with spacemen. 'Don't go out the front door.'

By the time Simon had checked his colt and was ready to leave, Bogart was already snoring hard.

There were, as far as they'd been able to find out during endless walks round the station, at least five doors that led into the mysterious interior. Bogart had guessed that it must be packed with equipment and medical apparatus, with immense racks of capsules of those frozen and ready for those about to be frozen. It was a reasonable assumption and Simon wondered if there was also living space for someone other than the crew, which seemed to number around thirty.

Simon had once seen round some experimental labs where the scientists were trying to freeze and then restore animals. With no success. The hardware they were using filled several big labs, with rows of freezing coils and containers. Plus the tissue and organ banks to cover any emergency failures. The interior of Paradise must be a masterpiece of space-saving and miniaturisation to get anywhere near enough equipment in there.

As always, the doors were guarded and locked. Simon had considered the direct attack, shooting their way past the sentries, but the risks were great, and he could foresee just how hard it would be to justify if he were wrong and it was a straight operation.

No. He still had to wait. Hoping that some miracle would come up and he'd find out who had the code and what they were going to do with it. The trouble was that there just didn't look like any obvious suspect. With the possible exception of Strafford, they could all have some sort of motive. And who knew even what darkness lurked in his heart? The most vicious killer Simon had ever encountered had looked like a Christian bishop and had loved children. Loved them so much that he had lured them away from their parents and then . . .

Singing from the lounge interrupted his thoughts. Chanting rather than singing, with muttered words thrown in. He'd thought that everyone was sleeping in their rooms.

The singing faded as he walked towards it, but he heard the vibrating and humming of the statues. Crooning gently, and in unison. There was only one person in the party who could have that sort of effect on the sonics, and that was the lady who'd

86

made them. Angelika Wellcome. Still drunk, by the sound of it.

She was such a quiet old lady, in her faded clothes and muted voice, that Simon always tended to overlook her. Yet, she had changed as much as Viki Laurel or Zeta Price. She had become morose and sad, drowning whatever plagued her mind with excesses of alcohol that surprised even a hardened drinker like Bogie.

Unnoticed, Simon crept silently into the lounge, sitting down in one of the deep, shadowed chairs, watching the eerie spectacle. A bottle of dark red liqueur stood three-quarters empty on one of the crystal tables, an overturned glass in a sticky puddle at its side.

The group of sculptures, spun from the finest metals and minerals, stood dazzling at the core of the room, their tones whistling and rising. Falling and sweeping in great runs of sound. The sonic sculpture had been known for many hundreds of years, invented by a lyric poet of Sol Three named Elias Ballard. But they had reached unbelievable heights of sophistication recently, being tuned by the experts to respond to any emotion.

The song they sang now was one of loneliness and death. A keening lament for something that had gone for ever and would never come again. Simon thought at first that it was a threnody for their creator, but why? If she were to rise again in the future, why should the sounds be so unbearably sad?

Angelika Wellcome half-sat, half-lay in one of the chairs that she'd dragged so it was directly under the main group of her statues. Eyes closed, oblivious to the fact that Simon had joined her, she waved her wrinkled hands to the rhythm of the statues, head shaking slowly backwards and forwards. And she was talking to them.

'Play on, lovelies. I can hear you right deep inside my head. Always could. Nobody like me for hearing you. Nobody makes you talk and sing like me. Isn't that right? Course it is. Course it is. Then he could as well. No! Not quiiiiiite as well as

Angelika. No he couldn't. But he was nice. So young and sooooooo nice.'

There was something chilling in the old woman's ramblings, with the long-drawn vowels stretching on and on. Simon sensed that he was hearing something deeply private. Something that she had never intended anyone to hear.

So he stayed.

'Too clever, wasn't he? Pretty boy. Pretty boy. Body like a god. Not so pretty in the furnace. Melted and spat like a hunk of rotten meat. Melted right away. Had to throw away that batch of greenstone. All spoiled by him.'

Was the old woman deranged, or was she thinking of some horror from her past? Simon stood up and moved closer, but she still ignored him. The sculptures didn't. They fell quieter, as though they were waiting to see what he did and said, before they reacted in any way.

She noticed the change in them, but kept her eyes closed, fingers falling to play with a heavy necklace of uncut amethysts that she wore.

'Has he come back?' she whispered. 'Is that it, my dear ones? Has he come back to haunt me again? Like he does every night. Naked and lovely. Sooooooo lovely. Thought he was clever and could take advantage of me, because my hands were going and I couldn't . . . But I could if I'd wanted! No. No. No. I could still make them sing. Still can, can't I, darlings? But not make them any more. He could. Couldn't you, darling boy? Use your hands, and we pretended they were still mine. Because I was the best. They all said so. Loved his as much as mine. I could tell the difference. He got so greedy. Cruel and rude to me. Laughed at me. At me! At Angelika Wellcome. Called me . . . called me names! I couldn't have that.'

'So you killed him?'

Simon's voice was quiet, barely ruffling the surface of the sonics, but it was enough to set them weeping. A dreadful jangling noise, like an infinity of bereaved children. The old

88

woman sat up as though she'd been immersed in freezing liquid already. Her eyes stood open in her head, and he could read the message in them. For a moment, he thought that she was going to pass out, but she rallied with a visible effort and tried to paste a smile on, but it fell away, and he saw only the trembling mouth of a frightened old woman.

'Commander! It's you! You made me start most dreadfully. I was just . . .'

The sentence petered out as she made an effort to remember just what she had been doing. Simon sat down alongside her, watching her face.

'I heard you. What you were saying. About the boy and how you killed him.'

She laughed at that. A high, thin, nervous laugh, riddled with falsehood that set the sculptures cheeping in a dreadful parody of the noise. Taking a deep breath, she tried one more time.

'I'm sorry, Commander. I'm tired and tomorrow's a big day.'

'The first day of the rest of your life, as Razan would put it.'

'Yes. Yes.' Eagerly. 'Well, I must have taken a little more wine than's good for me, so if you'll help me to . . .'

'Miss Wellcome. I'm sorry, but I heard what you said. I'm an officer in GalSec and I can't just forget it because you're old and ill and tomorrow you're due to be passed into a cryogenic coma. Murder is murder and there is no way in this galaxy that I can just walk round that.'

'No. You don't understand what happened.'

The note of desolation and despair hung heavy, almost silencing the statues.

'I'll tell you what happened, Miss Wellcome. Then you tell me I'm wrong and we'll forget it. Tell me I'm right and we go back to Crucis together.' She didn't speak.

'Right then. You're the best sculptor ever. They all say so. A few years ago it started to go. You could still make them sing for you. We've all heard that here. But not make them any more. So you got an assistant. Secretly. A young boy. How long ago was that?'

She spoke so quietly he couldn't hear.

'How long, Miss Wellcome?'

'Six years. Six years ago. He was such a lovely boy, Commander. Quite the most beautiful boy I'd ever seen. Everyone thought we were just lovers. My friends were so envious. It was ironic. We were never lovers. I used him and paid him very well. Later he came to use me.'

Simon nodded. 'He got better, and threatened to tell. Tell the world that the great Angelika Wellcome was a liar and a cheat and had been for years? So you killed him. Burned his corpse in your furnace and fled here, knowing that one day people would ask questions. But you wouldn't be there to answer them. You'd be safely asleep. Now, tell me, isn't that what happened?'

There was a hush in the lounge, as though even the statues waited to hear her deny it. Twice she opened her mouth, but no sound came out. Her head slumped forward on her chest and she began to cry. Great silent tears flowed over her wrinkled cheeks, splashing on the backs of her hands. Hands that had once produced some of the most beautiful sculptures in the world.

Simon sighed. 'I'm sorry. If it'll help, I won't tell anyone here. Just say that you've changed your mind about the freezing and come back to Crucis with us.'

'No. Please. I've got to go. I couldn't bear to go on living and know that people knew that all my work for so many years has been a lie. Please, let me go, Commander.'

To his great embarrassment, the old woman dropped to her knees in front of him, holding him round the legs, begging him to spare her the disgrace. She offered him money. Any of her statues. *All* of them. Just to let her go ahead with the freezing the next day.

Gently, he pushed her back, helping her to her feet. 'Miss Wellcome. You can't buy me. You can't threaten me. There's nothing that turns me aside. You killed someone and now you pay for it. That's the simple law. What happens will be affected by the fact that he tried to blackmail you.'

'Rehab at my age! That'd be a sorry joke. I will not come with you, Commander.'

'You must. There isn't any choice.'

'There is, and I will not. Those are my last words, Commander, and I bid you goodnight.'

He watched speechless as she walked carefully across the lounge, pausing to brush her hand softly over a small sonic by the door, that reacted with a purring sound almost like a stroked cat. Then she was gone.

Feeling inexpressibly depressed by what he had to do, Simon walked for an hour before finally going back to his own room and sleep.

Simon slept late, barely stirring when Bogie got up for his morning work-out in the gym. It seemed as though only a couple of minutes drifted by before Bogie was back, shaking him by the shoulder.

'What's the matter? You've only been gone a couple of minutes.'

'Right. I ran into Razan looking like he'd lost a diamond and found a shiny hunk of dreck. Bad news, Simon.'

'What?'

'Angelika Wellcome. The old lady wasted herself last night. Hung herself from a rail in her room, with the belt of her robe. Left a note, so Razan says.'

Simon got up and dressed quickly, buckling on his blaster as he walked to join the others in the lounge. Razan was there, pale and ghostly, looking like a living shadow. When Simon walked in, Razan stared at him with a venomous look, the eyes glittering among the crevices of bone.

'Again you bring death with you, Commander. You would do well in a necrology institute rather than a place dedicated to life.'

'Why did she do it, Simon?' The question came from Rafael Strafford, sitting alone on one side of the lounge. 'She seemed a harmless old lady. You wouldn't have been leaning on her, would you?'

'Yes, Mister Strafford, I did. I'm sorry to say that I had forbidden Miss Wellcome participation in the ceremony this afternoon. She would have accompanied my partner and I back to Crucis tonight to answer questions on the most serious charge possible.'

His statement was greeted with silence. Razan broke it. 'Her note said that you had denied her a chance. That you'd closed all the doors to hope.'

'No. She did that herself. Six years ago.'

'Well, I think . . .' began von Neumann.

'You know what I think of what *you* think. And all of you. I'm sorry she's dead, but she did kill someone, and being old doesn't mean that you get away with things just by saying sorry. I've had it with all of you.' Razan stood up, gathering his gown about him like a bird of prey tucking his wings in.

'I think we've heard enough. I accept what you say for the present, but I am bound to tell you that we . . . I am not entirely satisfied and I shall be forced to . . .'

He was talking and moving towards the door at the same time, until he ran into Bogart. Simon nodded imperceptibly to his partner.

'Hold it, Razan. I heard you say "we" when you meant to say "I". Who's this "we" all of a sudden? Getting rattled are we, Abraham? If your boss is so clever, why doesn't he just come out from back there and tell us so himself. Come on, Mister Thursby. The gig's up. Come and talk to us yourself.'

While Bogie blustered at the nervous giant, looking as though he might gather all his strength and leap up and hit him in the chest, Simon watched the others. And watched the guards, and watched the door to the perimeter corridor. Nothing happened.

Hand to ear, Razan tried to back away. 'No. You don't understand. It is in the contract that nobody who comes to Paradise shall try to find out . . .'

'We didn't sign any contract, Razan. Did we, Bogie?'

'No, Simon. And I think it's time that we saw this mysterious Floyd Thursby.' Bogie faced the blank wall, where he and Simon suspected there was some sort of vid monitor. 'Come out, come out, wherever you are. Time to give up gracefully.'

Simon was watching Razan, certain that the skinny man had some kind of transceiver, seeing the look of panic flit over his face as a contact seemed to be broken. He didn't see the door open behind him, but he heard the voice. Rich and full of good living.

'Give up, my dear Bogie. I tell you now, sir, that I'm a man not easily discouraged when I want something. But you'd both already know that. Wouldn't you?'

SEVEN

A FROZEN STIFF

It had been nearly ten years.

Simon's first serious mission. The first time he met Bogie. Back on the golden planet of Zayin.* There on the frontier world, dying before it had ever really lived, Simon had met this man before. Deep in the caverns where unguessable treasure had vanished for ever.

Now he was called Floyd Thursby.

Then he was called Harley Corman!

'Harley Corman!' Bogart took a step towards him, hand dropping to his colt, then paused as he saw that Simon hadn't moved.

'Yes. Or Floyd Thursby. For, as my dear old friend and mentor Casper Gutman once said. "What's in a name?" I break no law, do I?'

Simon watched him wonderingly, trying hard to think if there was still a call out on the fat man. Corman saved him the trouble.

'My dear young Simon. Let me set your mind at rest. There is no reason why your delightful Security Service would be interested in me now. All my youthful indiscretions are, happily, behind me. And the memory of the law may be long, but the statute of limitations within the Federation is mercifully short.'

That was true. Everything that was against Corman was

* See *Rack Three: Backflash.*

94

based on hearsay and rumour and supposition and coincidence. He had been seen near where a bomb might have gone off, or a fat man was staying in the city when jewels were stolen. Or a head of state might have had a grossly huge, jovial fellow as his last visitor before he was found with a crystal knife buried in his back.

Always Harley Corman.

Yet never Harley Corman.

Only that once, with Rack and Bogart, had he come close to being caught. Yet even then he'd somehow wriggled free. Simon felt a strange ambivalence towards Corman, whom he knew to be an unprincipled villain. Yet there was some quality of bravado and panache that he admired in the man. One could never imagine him doing anything small. That wasn't his nature.

Now here he was free. Running Paradise. Looking very little older than when Simon had last seen him on Zayin. Still vastly fat, eyes sharp as lasers among the rolls of flesh in his pink face. Still short of breath, panting even as he just stood there. Undoubtedly the man who'd tried to kill Simon in the corridor and slipped away. Still, from the look of his young friend, Kornelis, addicted to pleasures of the flesh that were far from heterosexual.

'Come, my dear young Simon Rack. You stand there as though the cat had got your tongue. Have you nothing to say to an old friend?'

'I have, Corman, and it's no friend you are. I say that I have waited, and that I will catch you yet. This operation might be straight. You've managed to convince a lot of people that it is. I don't think so.'

'Proof, my dear sir, is a commodity that rises in value with every day that passes. Do you possess any of it? No? I thought not. Then you would do well to trim your wings.'

'A man dead on the way here. A code stolen. Attempts on other lives. The bill mounts up.'

'And when my name appears on it, I shall gladly pay it.'

Now, he turned to face the others, standing fascinated by the tableau. 'I see you are puzzled by all this, as well you might be. I shall tell you all. I have no time for a man who holds his tongue. When he finally comes to talk, he will not know where to stop.'

'You are a criminal, Mister Corman. I have heard of you before.' Rafael Strafford peered closely at the fat man.

'And I.' It was von Neumann, shock scribbled all over his white face at the thought that this might be the last hurdle before new life, and he might yet fall at it.

'Me too,' said Zeta Price, soberly. 'A lot of men in the media business know your name. I've heard an awful lot of stories over the years.'

Corman chuckled. A fat, jolly sound, like bubbles being blown through honey. 'My dear people. You cannot have heard one half of one half of the tales that I have heard about myself. And I regret that some of them might have been true. But that was long ago. Ask the Commander here if he has heard of me in the last many years.'

'He's been quiet. That doesn't mean he's been keeping clean. Just he hasn't been caught.'

'Tut, tut. You beat me fairly and squarely at our last meeting, Simon, my dear boy. I hold no grudge. I would be saddened to find that you had turned into a bad winner. That's a creature one step worse than a bad loser. Since then, I have been quite clean, devoting my not inconsiderable talents to this work in hand. And now it has reached fruition. I would regret if it were to be spoiled by petty hatred over a misspent youth. As Casper Gutman would say; I may have changed my spots, but that does not mean I can no longer hunt.'

The steel beneath the jolly exterior showed through for a second, and Simon remembered what a dangerous man Corman was to underrate.

'What about us? Does this mean it's all off?'

'My sweet gal. Miss Laurel, isn't it?' Corman waddled over

to where the vid-star sat, and leaned over her, pressing her hand to his lips. The effect made him pant even more, and he wiped sweat from his dome of a forehead before going on.

'The motto of Floyd Thursby Enterprises, though we can now call it Harley Corman Enterprises, is "New Life For Old". That is what you have signed up for, and that is what you'll get. This afternoon, after we have all dined together, I shall personally escort you to your capsules, to take what my good friend and manager of Paradise, Razan, would call the first moments of an eternity of tomorrows. Are there any questions from any of you?'

He was good. Very good indeed, thought Simon. He'd pulled the rug from under the feet of some of the richest and most powerful men and women in the galaxy. Admitted it. Then dusted them down and said we're going on. And nobody was going to object.

'Yes. I want it made clear that I allow this to go on only on the understanding that if there is one more untoward happening, I stop it and we all go back to Crucis for a long talk.'

Corman turned to the others, a great smile lighting up his features. 'There,' he said, as proudly as though Simon were his favourite son. 'I always say that I like a man who says what he means. Very well, my dear boy. I shall do everything in my power to ensure that nothing else goes amiss with my operation. Won't we, Abraham?'

Taken by surprise at the sudden question, the lean man jumped visibly, stammering out his agreement with his master's voice.

'What happens now? Why can't we get on with it now, instead of waiting till later? That way there won't be any foul-ups.' Von Neumann was in a pitiable state, sweat beading his head, fingers tangling with each other and plucking at his clothes. Every other breath he gasped at a sudden pain, obviously finding it an effort merely to stay upright.

Corman smiled gently at him. 'My dear Karl. You have

waited all of your life for today. I think you can wait just a little longer. Don't you? I'm sure that you do. We will have a pleasant lunch together and then all go to the cryogenics lab refreshed and ready to face our bright future.'

'Like a last supper, but a few hours early? Count me out of it, Corman. I eat when I want and choose who with.'

Bogie's curt refusal didn't seem to put the fat man out at all. 'Of course. You always were a man of your own impulse, Bogie. I like that in you. Admire it. I only hope it doesn't, one day, cause you any inconvenience. Is there anyone else who prefers not to dine with us?'

Nobody answered. Simon guessed that Bogie planned to have a last try at getting in the back door and that if he also opted from the meal it would put Corman more on his guard. Since there was no objection, Harley Corman was about to lead them away from the lounge when a voice came from the back.

'I think that I would rather not join you, Mister Corman. I feel very tired, and shocked after my husband's death. If you'll excuse me?'

'But of course. Of course. Of course we will, my very dear Ruth. We understand the strain you've been through in the last few days. We understand it better than you could ever imagine. But, I must take you to task on one thing, Ruth. Wallace, your dearly beloved one, is not dead. As an ancient poet once put it, he is not dead, he is merely sleeping. A sleep that will also come to you in a matter of a few hours, and then you will be with him again. For all of eternity.'

He knew about them. Simon was sure of it in the way he spoke. He must have bugs around Paradise, picking up scraps of information. The spin-offs could provide him with a nice little sideline. Yet, somehow that wasn't like Harley Corman. Whatever else he might be, it was no picker-up of trifles under the tables of the rich and powerful. That wouldn't pay the initial capital outlay of Paradise. Nowhere near, never mind the massive operating costs.

Either it was straight, which he suspected it was, or there was something more. Maybe something wrapped up in a little gold capsule.

The meal was superb, with the food-preps pulling out all the stops. Everyone could have exactly what they wanted. Strafford made a wry joke about it.

'We condemned men are going to get a hearty breakfast. Is that it, Corman?'

The fat man had joined in the general laughter at his own expense. Simon noticed the tension underlying the meal, with everyone except the negro edgy and nervous, ready to laugh too easily. Too often there were uneasy silences, though Corman was always ready to break them with an amusing tale from his chequered past.

It was interesting to see what they each chose to eat. Despite the incredible range of food offered, most of them went for simple meals. Viki Laurel asked for an omelette, and a green salad on the side. Zeta Price wanted a big steak, medium rare. Von Neumann chose a thick stew, and piles of vegetables – things that his diet denied him. Strafford went for soul food, tucking into a plate of pigs' feet and black-eyed peas.

Simon was the exception. Chances of eating well came rarely to field operators in GalSec and he and Bogie had been eating well, if not too wisely. He went for salmon, followed by Sole Walewska with a green salad. Chateaubriand steak and all the trimmings followed by the finest soufflé he'd ever had. By the time he'd reached the cheese course, he was feeling just a little overfull.

But apart from the simple desire to make the most of his last opportunity on Paradise, it was also important to Bogie that he buy him as much time as possible. By dragging the meal through all its courses, Simon bought him nearly two hours. As he sipped at the Turkish coffee, he wondered how he'd used the time.

Bogie had gone first to his room, changing into his working uniform, feeling happier in it than in the flowing robes of Paradise. The colt was back in its accustomed holster. Taking a deep breath, ignoring the superb smells that were drifting from the food-prep rooms, Bogie crept out of his suite, padding along the deserted corridor, through the lounge, where the sonic sculptures now stood silent, as though they mourned Angelika Wellcome, towards the corridor where Simon had been attacked.

He saw Razan, arm drooped round the shoulder of Kornelis, a few paces ahead of him, and he dropped back until they'd vanished round the next corner. He guessed that they were going to a room that he and Simon had sussed out was the staff eaterie. With the freezing coming up, they'd decided that there might be a lot of preparation round the labs, leaving the rest of the station more vulnerable to inspection.

Pausing for a moment, Bogie stood still and listened. Ahead of him was one of the secret doors, always with its guard. If he was there, standing up near a display cabinet filled with precious jewels from all over the galaxy, then Bogie had already decided he was going to have to be moved. If that meant wasting him, then he'd get wasted. Time was too short and the prize too big for drawing back now.

He poked his head cautiously round the corner, conscious of how loud his own breathing sounded in the stillness. There was nobody there. The sentry on the door to the men's eaterie had stood rigidly still as Bogie'd gone past, smiling vaguely at him, muttering some comment to the man about taking a last trip around.

It had worked. The guard wasn't there on the door. That made it a hell of a . . . He stopped, seeing something sticking

100

out beyond the cabinet. And then noticing something else on the floor. Something that might have looked like a string of rubies, pouring out their rich colour across the white carpet.

But it wasn't rubies.

In vids, people always stopped and dipped their fingers in suspicious pools when they saw them. Bogie didn't need to. He'd seen enough blood in his life to be absolutely certain of what it looked like. Stepping over the trickle of red, already soaking into the carpet, Bogie found the river from which the stream flowed. And the pool that was the outlet for the river.

The sentry was dead. Not all the medics and freezing in the galaxy would bring him back to life. Someone had got up really close to him and used a slicer on him. That was a small hand gun, much favoured by whores on frontier worlds as bag protection, that fired a small disc of metal, rather like a tiny circular saw. Although a slicer was notoriously inaccurate over a range of more than two metres, its effect on the human abdomen was devastating.

It ripped in, and then carried on spinning until its teeth became choked with blood and bone. The guard had no chance. His gun was still holstered, and his face contorted with the appalling agony of the slicer blade tearing out his stomach.

Bogie sniffed, looking down at the shambles of blood and intestines. 'Rehabs never did have any guts,' he muttered as he stepped over the body, careful not to get his boots slobbered with the thick blood, colt in hand, pushing open the door.

It wasn't locked, swinging silently at his touch.

At that moment, Simon was just making the first fine cut in the firm meat of his sole, peeling it away from the bone, dipping it in the Mornay sauce, then in the rich lobster butter.

The door led to a narrow corridor, undecorated with any sort of picture or hanging, and obviously designed to be totally functional. The walls were bare plasteel, with no doors opening off them. Bogie stalked along, sniffing at the warm air, noting that the scents that were pumped into Paradise were conspicuous here only by their absence. The lighting was dim and intermittent, making it hard to see far ahead.

It was an uneasy feeling, knowing that if anyone else came into the corridor from either end, there wouldn't be any way of keeping out of sight. And it couldn't take long before someone found the butchered corpse of the sentry. Then, there was a door right ahead, nearly closed.

Bogie applied his eye to the slit, peering round the corner, expecting to see . . . what? He didn't really know. Perhaps some massive freezing plant, or a room filled with complex laboratory equipment. Racks filled with capsules, each with its frozen inhabitant.

Certainly not Ruth Gironde, sitting on the edge of a large table, swinging a leg and singing to herself.

The steak was perfect, done exactly as he'd hoped, and the vegetables a million miles away from the sticky reprocessed mush served in the GalSec canteens. Corman was in the middle of a strange tale about a jewelled dragon he'd once spent seventeen years chasing after. The rest of the guests were interested in spite of themselvs, and Simon marvelled once again at the mystery that was Harley Corman.

On the table, tubes dangling from it like the intestines of a dead insect, lay the pod that had contained the earthly remains of Wallace Gironde. There was a panel in the wall, filled with plugs and sockets, lights flickering in a mad symphony of colour.

From where he was, Bogart couldn't see if Gironde still slumbered in the capsule, but it certainly had his name on. A thought struck him about all the tubes that dangled limply to the floor. They were the life-support system that they'd seen pumping all the nutrients and keeping the freezing mixture at the right temperature. If they hung like that, not connected to anything, what was keeping Wallace Gironde alive now?

'Nothing' is the short and simple answer to that.

Moving slowly, so as not to make her jump, Bogie stepped into the room. Ruth turned round and smiled brightly at him. 'Well, how nice to see you. Have you come to bury me now?'

That didn't seem the sort of comment that he'd anticipated, but Bogie ignored it, walking over to the capsule. He really expected to find that his suspicions were wrong, and that there'd be a halo of mist and ice round the sleeping face of Wallace Gironde.

There was a halo. But it was the pale ghost of corruption already working. In the warm atmosphere of the station, decay wasn't held long at bay. The soft tissues of the eyes were already turning milky and rotting. The flesh was waxy and slightly swollen. *Rigor mortis* was evident. And the casket wasn't even cool.

'Will you bury me with him? Close the lid of the capsule on us both?' She laughed lightly at the thought. 'Then he can hold me for ever, till his fingerbones stick through his finger-ends, pinning me to him for ever. He won't forget, you know.'

Bogart knew two truths at that moment. That Gironde was dead. Not a frozen stiff, but a mouldering corpse. Probably dead from heart failure. Dead when they all filed past the capsule and stared through the icy mist at the wonders of cryogenic science. And the second thing was that Ruth Gironde was mad.

That left a priority. To get out and warn Simon that the whole thing was beginning to smell like a fix.

'Bogart? It's you.' The voice was suddenly normal, pitched uncomfortably loud.

'Yes, it's me. I really think we ought to get out of this place. Now.'

'Yes. He's dead, you know. Wallace. They tricked me, didn't they?'

A sudden alternative possibility occurred to Bogie. Simon had told him about freezing experiments, where bodies were kept without any visible signs of decay for months. But the moment you pulled the switch and brought the temperature and everything else back to normal, then the flesh began to mortify at a horrific speed. Like the ending of some of the vampire vids they ran sometimes on the late night.

If Ruth Gironde had come in here, having killed the guard, then she could have pulled the switch in a moment of blind hatred, forgetting the effect that would have on her lover's life. He shuddered at the thought. That raised all manner of different problems. Either way, it was going to mean that the cryogenics scheduled for this afternoon weren't going to take place. Either someone had let Gironde die, or his wife had murdered him. Neither possibility would slip by, once Simon heard about them.

'I wanted him and he wanted me then I didn't want him but he still wanted me and then I wanted someone else and he still wanted me and then he knew I didn't want him and part of him stopped wanting me but he wouldn't let go. Wouldn't let go. Wouldn't let go.'

The monologue became a droning chant, her voice lilting and falling. Becoming louder. Bogie looked round the room. There was another door on the other side of the room, but it was firmly closed.

'Ruth. Come on. Let's go. We'll talk about it later. Hurry up or they'll find the guard and we're all in the . . . just hurry up.'

Her eyes turned to him, and he saw the pupils dilated with shock. Or dope. Or both. 'I saw the man dead, lying in a pool of blood. I saw him, Bogie.' She seemed normal again, but there was no way of knowing how long that state would last. 'I

104

couldn't believe that Wallace was gone. I had to look, and I came in and found him like this.'

'The guard was already dead? And these tubes were already disconnected?'

The thought brought him up short. There were so many possibilities to consider that his brain filled at the thoughts. If she hadn't . . .

'And now he's dead. Any way now, any day now. Once the word gets back to Wallace's men, the contract'll go out. Would I look good in a long black veil, Reverend? It'll suit my heart, will it not, where the blackness of despair lies like the weight of all time.'

She was gone again. Bogie took her by the arm and started to pull her away. Ruth resisted a little, looking up at him with the beginning of fear.

'Why are you taking me away? I wanted to look at Wallace and make sure he was all right. If he's not . . . but he is. Everything's all right, isn't it?'

'Yes. Everything's just fine.'

Most of the guests had drifted away from the table, leaving Corman, Strafford and Simon. Rack put down his cup, empty at last. If Bogie hadn't done it by now, then it would be time for desperate measures. Moving the saucer, he noticed that a little of the bloody gravy from his steak had splashed on the crisp, white linen. Absently, he scratched at it with a finger-nail. It shifted, leaving a small, red stain.

Ruth Gironde walked in front of him down the dull-walled corridor. Bogie constantly turned to the rear, expecting to hear shouts when they found that Gironde wasn't frozen any more. Just an ordinary stiff.

At the end, the door was pushed shut, so that they couldn't see the body of the sentry any more. A thread of the bright blood had run under the door, like some sinister alien life-form trying to gain entrance to the interior of the station.

'Bogart?'

'What?'

The voice sounded normal, but her mood changed so fast that it was difficult to follow. 'After I'm frozen, will you do something for me? Will you try and find a friend for me and help him?'

'Simon said that if Wallace died, that your "friend" might be wasted.'

Brightly: 'Yes, but Wallace isn't dead, is he? So that's all right.'

The shock made reality hard to bear, and she seemed to be retreating into her own chosen alternative future. Bogie shook his head, reaching past her to push the door open.

Where Razan was waiting with a needle-gun pointed at them. Bogie reacted instantly, slamming the door, feeling the jolt as the skinny giant fired at them. He was getting ready to back away, hoping to find a way out through the cryogenic core of the station, when he heard another voice behind him.

'Don't move!'

There was the chilling snout of a needle-gun pressed into Bogie's spine. By the voice and the scent of perfume, he guessed that it was the hesher, Kornelis.

'In a place like this, you shouldn't say: "Don't move." You should just say: "Freeze!"'

EIGHT

A CHILLING CLIMAX

The meal was over.

All the guests had departed from the lounge for a last hour of solitary meditation with themselves before they would come back for one final time to make their farewells. Corman had gone, vanished into the interior, and Razan hadn't been seen for some hours.

Alone in the deep chair, momentarily regretting that he'd eaten so much, Simon sat and waited for Bogie to report back to him. If he didn't bring good news, then it was all going to be up to him to pull a miracle out of his hat. And right at that moment, he felt that he was fresh out of miracles.

'Commander? I thought that I should find you here. The others have all said that they would like to bid you a fond farewell as well as each other. I like that, my dear Simon. I like that very much.'

With a gasping sigh, Corman flopped down into one of the chairs alongside him, looking like a great mythical whale in his billowing white robes. He dabbed at beads of sweat on his face with a cambric handkerchief, smiling round it at Rack.

'Upon my soul, Simon, I had never thought to see you again after that calamity on Zayin.'

'How did you escape, Corman?'

'Aha.' He rubbed the side of his nose with a wink. 'There are ways out of most things, my dear young friend.'

'Except this one. One of the men and women on that shuttle is a murderer and a thief. Have you got the genetic code, Corman?'

Although the fat man was an actor of consummate skill, he seemed to Simon to be genuinely shocked. 'My dear boy, I have always admired your talent for jumping to a conclusion and sometimes finding the right one. But really! You know what I do.'

'Rob, murder, plan and plot. Tell me what you don't do, Corman.'

Confidentially, Harley leaned nearer to him, placing a monstrously chubby finger to his lips. 'Between you and I, dear Simon, I have to confess to a certain smattering of truth in that allegation. But have you known me go in for these international plots and secrets of the galaxy? Casper Gutman would spin in his urn if he thought I'd got involved in that sort of affair. One meets such a poor and vicious class of person in that game. Oh, no.'

Simon could almost have believed him. Almost. 'Fair enough. Then, what do you want here? Haven't you got anything better to do?'

'No. Just wished to have a little of the pleasure of your company. And to find out if you were serious about your threat to close us down if there's a bit more trouble.'

Simon stood up, running his hands over the dead shapes of the statues, feeling them stir slightly, giving off a faint hum. 'Fair question, Corman. Yes. One more incident, and it's off. But there's only an hour to go. You worried that something might happen at the last moment, like in the vids? Maybe that I'll call all the suspects together here and break them down with a brilliant speech that'll have the guilty one sobbing for mercy at my feet? Come on, now.'

'I confess that I find you a great source of pleasure, my dear Simon. I have watched your career with interest, from . . . well, let us say from wherever my work took me over the last few years. When I received the request for two GalSec officers to come here on a secret mission, I somehow felt that it would be you and the admirable Bogart. Now things have gone somewhat awry.' He ticked them off on his fingers. 'Bulman dead. Secret lost. The elderly lady putting herself away. Someone trying to kill you and poor Bogart. And Gironde . . . being frozen early.'

Just for a moment, Simon thought that Corman had intended to say something different about Gironde, and changed his mind. He glanced down at his kron. Only forty minutes till they all went off to the labs.

'Can I not persuade you to try our little techniques? Perhaps a six-month sleep would do you good, my dear Simon. The world of good.'

'No. I'll take an ice-check on that one.' Where the hell was Bogie? He should have been back an hour ago.

Corman levered himself out of the depths of the chair, like a leviathan surfacing. He stood for a second or two, straining to recover his breath. 'Will you walk with me around Paradise, Simon? You'll make an old man very happy if you do. I always find these last few minutes something of a strain on the nerves.'

Rack was just about to agree, when he changed his mind. 'Sorry, Corman. Haven't seen Bogie for some time. Better dig him up.'

With a wave of the hand, he walked out of the lounge, leaving Harley staring thoughtfully after him. The moment he'd gone, Corman, moving with surprising ease for such a huge man, ran to one of the secret doors into the interior and vanished.

The ship seemed cooler than before. Simon went first to their room, in case Bogart had slipped back and fallen into one of his 'short' naps. The room was empty. Bogie's uniform was gone, and his colt. There was something wrong. If he wasn't there, he'd have made some effort to get in touch with Simon to give him any news. He hadn't, so that meant something had changed his plans. And that something could only be bad.

Quickly, Simon also threw off the clinging robes of Paradise, pulling on the uniform, strapping his blaster in place. Checking that the para-charge was full, he went first to the lounge again, in case Bogie had come back while he'd been away. It was still and empty.

As far as he could see, the station was deserted. The main doors into the interior were all unguarded, something that had never happened in all the previous week. Simon tested them with his shoulder, but they were locked tight shut. The perimeter corridor was deserted and silent, though he once thought he heard a woman's voice raised behind one of the tapestries. When he paused, the sound, if there'd been any sound, had stopped.

Round the next corner, he stopped again. The strip of white carpeting had been altered in some way. A new band of dirtier material had been laid down across the . . . No, it wasn't that. The dirty was the existing carpet. It stood out in contrast to a new strip of cleaner white. That hadn't been there the last time. Simon was sure of that. It would have registered as something out of the ordinary. He bent down and looked carefully at it.

It was just outside one of the semi-hidden doors, near where someone had shot at him. Eyes flicking to make sure nobody was coming, he knelt down, rubbing his finger over the join between the two pieces of thick white carpet. Using the blade of his knife he succeeded in levering up the one edge, revealing the plasteel floor underneath. It was clean.

Not the least trace of any kind of dirt or dust, like you normally found round the edges of any carpet, even the new anti-stat-repellent ones. The floor had been cleaned carefully and scrupulously. Why? What had been on the floor and on the carpet that they'd so hurriedly removed the stained material *and* cleaned the smooth surface underneath?

Face thoughtful, Simon stood up, the colt now in his hand. The rest of the perimeter brought him nothing, other than the faintest of glows back towards Crucis that told him that the next shuttle was on its way. Not a hint of Bogart's presence. Finally, he found himself back in the lounge, where Corman was waiting for him.

'You've been searching for something?'

'Bogie? Where is he?'

'Ah, yes. Come, come now, my dear Simon, neither of us think that Bogart is not capable of looking after himself. I'm sure he'll turn up. Have you looked in all the rooms? I believe that he was fond of both the pools and the gym.'

'He wouldn't just vanish at a time like this. Not unless . . .'

'Unless what?'

'Unless someone was stopping him from coming back here. Someone like you, Corman, or one of your hesher minions.'

'Now, that is not a pleasant thing to say, Simon. I find that rather hurtful. Perhaps I might offer you an alternative "unless" to think about.'

Corman was smiling gently at him, like a jolly uncle who's managed to catch out a favourite nephew with a little trick.

'Go on, Corman. Pull it out of your sleeve and lay it on the table.'

'Very well, sir. Very well. Your comrade is not the only one of our little party who seems to have gone missing. There is another, Simon. Another.'

Simon remembered the noise of a woman's voice, crying behind the tapestry. 'Viki Laurel? Or Ruth Gironde?'

'You guess a woman, immediately. Might not Bogart have gone to share some kind of pleasure with a man? No? No, I assume that you are correct. Though one never . . . Still, let it pass. It is the widowed Ruth Gironde who seems to have disappeared.'

Rack wondered in passing about the use of that word 'widow'. Razan had always taken great pains never to link the freezing process with death. Gironde wasn't dead. Merely sleeping away the time until he could be revived to face the

111

delightful prospect of immortality.

Corman watched him, seeing how the news might take him. It *was* possible, just possible, that Ruth Gironde had cracked at the last and asked Bogie to help her, and that he'd found some way of getting into the interior of the station and hiding them both there. But only if it didn't jeopardise the mission. So? There wasn't anything to do. Just wait and see how the dice rolled for him.

'Simon, my dear boy. You don't seem, if I may make so bold as to suggest this, you don't seem surprised at the idea.'

'Corman. Bogie's a big boy now. He doesn't need me to hold his hand for him.'

Corman looked at an ornate kron on his fat wrist, exclaiming with surprise. 'Goodness! How time speeds by when one is enjoying a friend's company. It is time for the guests to be saying their farewells. They should be nearly through, and then they will each come in here to make their departures from both of us. I do so hope that Ruth Gironde isn't late. I hate the idea of trying to reclaim the penalty credits from a young woman in that sorry situation. Still.' He sighed.

A door opened on the far side of the lounge, nearest to the guests' rooms, and the skeletal figure of Razan appeared. He was wearing a gown of silver, hair tied back with a gleaming band of gold. His eyes were still masked by the odd glittering, deep within the canyons of his face.

'The shuttle will be docking late, as we feared. The new guests will not be able to see the freezing take place, but I have arranged for the whole ceremony to be vidded to be shown later. Perhaps tonight.'

Corman bowed his appreciation of his man's thought. 'That is excellent, Abraham. If the others are ready, then you can show them in here. One at a time, I think would be more tasteful and discreet.'

Razan inclined his head on his towering shoulders and walked out again, closing the door silently behind him. Corman watched him go, then faced Simon.

'I searched a long time for that man. I wanted someone with a superb presence. A wonderful speaking voice, like a cathedral organ. And I found him.' He grinned and nudged Simon with a fleshy elbow. 'Trouble is, my dear boy, that he hasn't the brains of a flea. If I weren't here, then the whole thing would fall apart. Fortunately, I have young Kornelis to keep an eye on things.'

'But he was frozen for six months,' said Simon, surprised at the mention of the hesher.

'Quite. Quite so. But he was actually only frozen for some of the time.' He seemed flustered at the mistake. If it was a mistake. 'Anyway, Razan is little more than an adequately functioning puppet for whom I have to tug the strings.'

'You've got a transceiver on him for you to talk to him. In his hair, just behind the ear. At first I thought it was a transplant.'

Corman chuckled, genuinely amused. 'Upon my soul, Simon. Upon my soul! And I thought that nobody would ever rumble my little ruse. You are uncommonly sharp, dear boy. Uncommonly sharp.' He leaned forwards. 'Simon Rack, I would dearly like to have you along. You're a man of nice judgement and many resources.'

Any reply that Simon might have been about to make was shut back in his throat, by the opening of the door and the appearance of Zeta Price. The little man wore a gown of plain yellow, and his hair was clipped and grey. He was bare-footed. Whatever else Paradise might have done to some of the others, it had undoubtedly changed the vid-commentator for the better. All the loudness was gone, and he came forward and shook Corman by the hand.

Turned to Simon and also shook his hand. 'Commander. I'm grateful to you for all that your service has done in the past. I regret somewhat one or two of my earlier broadcasts on the subject of the Galactic Security Service. When I wake again, I assure you I shall be more careful. It has been a most beneficial experience. I hope that you find that missing code. I only wish that I could help you. Goodbye.'

As soon as he'd gone, von Neumann stalked in. He had chosen a sober robe of grey, with a thin line of silver trimming down the front. Very much the discreet attire for the retiring diplomat. He exchanged a few words with Corman, then turned and shook hands formally with Simon. It seemed as if he wasn't going to speak, then he coughed twice.

'Commander. We will not, I think, ever meet again. I am sorry for the differences that there have been between us. I have been in . . . You understand, I think. Goodbye, Commander. I trust your mission will end well.'

Simon smiled. 'And I wish you the same. Good luck on your journey.'

Viki Laurel ran in next, smiling at both of them. Her hair was its natural colour, shining over her bare shoulders. The gown she'd chosen was scarlet, edged with tiny green gemstones that shimmered as she walked. Like Price, she was barefoot. Her skin glowed with health, and she looked a different woman from the painted, simpering vid-star who'd climbed aboard the shuttle seven days before. Paradise had also been good for her.

She flung her arms round Corman and, to Simon's amusement, kissed him on both cheeks. Winking over her shoulder at Simon, the fat man kissed her back, wishing her good fortune. Eyes sparkling with excitement, she went to Simon and hugged him, pressing her soft lips to his, hot little tongue pushing insistently at his mouth, sucking his tongue into the sexual cavern of her mouth. Grinding her lips against his, pressing her body to him, so that he could feel her nakedness and be aware of the response in himself.

Suddenly she pulled away from him, panting. 'Simon Rack. I must go, otherwise I'll never want to be frozen. Not when you warm me up like that. If Mister Corman agrees, maybe you can

114

come up here in six months when I'm out and you can help thaw me after that nasty cold capsule.'

She shuddered at the thought of the lonely darkness, then shook it off. 'I'm happy for knowing you, Simon. When I come out, I'd like to get to know you better and longer.'

He put his hands on her shoulders, fingers digging lightly into her soft flesh. 'Maybe, Viki. Wait and see how you feel when you come out. You'll go back to vids?'

'Perhaps. I don't know. Paradise has made me think about a lot of things.' She came closer and whispered in his ear: 'You won't let on about me not really being ill, will you, darling?'

'No. No, I won't. Come on now. You're going to be keeping everyone waiting.'

'Till we meet again, Simon,' she said, running over to the door and vanishing through it.

'Goodbye, Viki,' he said, knowing that she was already too far away to hear it.

Last of the survivors was Rafael Strafford. Wearing purple, unrelieved by any other colour. Smiling at Corman he shook his hand and said the usual formal words of thanks that any-one would say after a pleasant stay or a fine party. Finally he faced Simon, clasping his hand in a firm grip.

'Commander Rack. Simon. It has been a pleasure being here and knowing you. I am only deeply sorry that your time on Paradise has been unhappy, tainted with failure and death. There will be other days. Better days. Incidentally, I have done what I can, but I am no nearer than you to solving the mystery of the empty capsule. Genetics never were a great interest in my life. One of the things that I shall do when I finally wake from my sleep is to dig back into the distant past and look up to see whether Commander Rack, as he then was, successfully solved the mystery of Paradise. Goodbye, Simon.'

'Rafael, if I don't solve this one, then you may never get to wake up at all. Good luck.'

With a wave, Strafford walked over to the door, pausing and

looking back at them. A thought struck Simon, and he called across: 'Rafael?'

'Yes.'

'One question. You're healthy, successful, rich. Why are you here?'

'I was tired of things, Simon. So what do you do when you get tired? You fall asleep. It seems a good idea. Goodbye, Simon.'

'Goodbye.'

The door closed for the last time. Corman patted him on the arm. 'Come now. Let us go and see them as they journey into that far unknown. Take the dark ferry across the black waters.'

'I thought the dark ferry was only when you died, Harley?'

Corman didn't answer, turning as the door from the perimeter corridor was flung open and Ruth Gironde walked in.

Like the others she was wearing a loose robe. A pale blue, trimmed with a darker blue. Her hair was a tangled mat of spun silk, collapsing over her neck and shoulders. She wore no make-up, her face pale, eyes staring vaguely at the two men.

Although she was looking at Simon, Corman moved fast across the thick carpet to take her arm. 'My dear Sister Ruth. We were all so worried about you. We thought that you weren't going to join us. I am so glad.'

Her body went rigid as he touched her, hands still clasped firmly behind her. Corman tried to edge her across the lounge towards the other door, where the guests had gone on their way to the cryogenic labs. But she resisted him, pulling back towards Simon.

'Let her go, Corman. Something's wrong. She's in deep shock. Look at her face.'

Breathing heavily, Harley continued to hang on to her arm. 'My dear Simon,' he panted. 'I have been here for six months and I have seen this reaction several times. It is the spirit fighting to remain free from the bonds of endless sleep. It will pass and she will thank us for it. Come. Help me get her to the labs.'

Ruth made a harsh sound, deep in her throat, and suddenly threw her arms wide, sending Corman, for all of his size, staggering back. Her hands were held out, parallel to the floor, fingers stretched straight. Simon closed his eyes for a moment at the sight, fearing that it meant death for someone. And that the death could well be Bogart's.

Her hands were smothered with blood. Masked in red, dabbled from the tips of her fingers to the wrists, and smeared high up her arms. It looked as though she'd immersed both hands in a tub of blood, trying to wash away some unimagined sin.

'Sister!' exclaimed Corman, hands fluttering at the air in indecision.

'Ruth. What's happened?'

As quickly as the tension had seized her, it left her, and she sank down in a chair, looking at her arms as though they'd been grafted on to her without her knowledge. Looked from Simon to Corman and back.

'Simon. My hands. The blood. Whose is it? I went to see Wallace. Oh, Krishna! ! There's so much death! ! !'

The last word was screamed at the top of her voice. Like an actor on cue, an assistant appeared through the door from the labs. And was waved back by Corman. As the door closed, the other one opened and in came Razan, his silver robe splashed with streaks of red, his hair loose in its golden band. When he saw Ruth Gironde, he stopped, looked at Corman.

'Later, Abraham,' said Corman gently to him. 'Sister Ruth is about to tell us herself.'

'But . . . She's . . .'

'I said wait. In good time. Stay there and be ready if I need you. Ruth. Tell us what happened.'

Simon moved towards the seated woman, kneeling on the

floor by her feet. 'Ruth. It's Simon. Tell me. Where's Wallace? And where's Bogie?'

'Dead. All of them dead. No.' There was a long silence, broken only by Corman's ragged and irregular breathing, close behind him. Simon stared at the distraught woman, resting his hands in her bloodstained fingers.

'Please, Ruth.'

'It's all fine. Everything. I've come here so that I can be frozen with my husband. That was why I came here in the first place. I don't want anything to stop that happening. It would be too . . . too . . .'

She began to cry.

'My dear Simon. It is essential to the timing of the operation that nothing holds it up. Abraham will take her to the labs and we will follow and find out what has happened.'

'Bogie could be dead.' Simon turned round to look at Corman, catching him staring intently at Razan. Taking them both by surprise, Simon jumped up and leaped at the skinny man, drawing his colt as he did, pushing it up against the giant's throat. 'Tell me who's dead, you bastard. Or I'll kill you like a dog!'

The venom was so great that Razan almost passed out, eyes open wide. 'Not Bogie. Jerzy. Kornelis. She killed him with a knife and got away.'

There.

It was out. Slowly, Simon turned round to Corman, the colt steady on the big man's gross stomach. 'That's it, Harley. Stop the game right now. Send the order to stop everything and get them all back in here.'

'Simon. My dear . . .'

'Nothing, Harley. This is on kill, and I'll put a charge through your guts just like that. Your man says Ruth's killed your boy. Killed the hesher and got away. Away from what, Corman? And where's Bogie? Why hasn't he got away?'

The woman, ignoring the drama that had exploded about

her, stood up and smiled at Simon. 'Dear Commander Rack. What can you be talking about? Nobody's dead. Nobody.' Her voice trembled at the lie.

'That on your hands . . . Cranberry sauce, Ruth? Come on. You and Bogie found something back inside. The hesher caught you and you killed him. Escaped. Bogie didn't. What about Wallace? Is he alive or dead?'

'Alive, of course. What a silly idea, Simon. Everyone's alive. And now we're all going to go to sleep and when we wake up it'll all be over. And you mustn't stop us.'

'Yes. I must.'

Her mouth open in a soundless scream, Ruth hurled herself at Simon, taking him by surprise, hanging on to his gun-hand, nearly knocking him over. It took him less than a second to pull her from him. But that was at least a half second too slow. Both Razan and Corman had drawn needle-guns, pointing them at him.

'Now, my dear Simon, I suggest that you place that nasty toy on the floor and that Abraham will then take the lady to the laboratory, where she can be kept quiet. You and I will go and see what has happened to poor dear Kornelis. Such a sweet and wilful boy. Then we will see what we will see and we shall hear what we shall hear.'

Simon grinned mirthlessly at the fat man. 'Trouble with this place is that everyone keeps blowing hot and cold.'

Corman laughed.

NINE

RESTFUL FAREWELLS

At least Simon had managed to see behind the scenes on Paradise. Although it would have been better under different circumstances. With Corman keeping a careful three paces behind him, he was taken through the hidden door and along the narrow corridor. Through a small ante-room with a bank of clicking lights on one wall and then through the grey door opposite into a room the size of which took him by surprise.

Allowing for the quarters for the crew and the eating and sleeping space, virtually the whole of the hub of the station was occupied by this one central chamber. It was clearly the nerve centre of the operation, with functional panels that controlled the heating and lighting of the station and another for entry and exit ports and gravity control.

There was a row of five padded seats along one wall, facing a bank of vids that simultaneously showed views of different parts of Pararise. Although all of them had speakers linked in, they'd been turned right down and there was just a constant background flow of murmurs, the words inaudible.

As they entered the room, Abraham Razan came in through another door opposite, obviously from the other side of the station. From the cryogenic labs. One thing about the set-up puzzled Simon. From what they'd seen when the earlier guests were being processed, the actual room where the freezing took place was quite small and virtually empty of any scientific equipment. And since this chamber was as big as it was, then where were the storage quarters for the chilled bodies of the previous six months' guests?

The gun prodded him in the back, and Simon took a couple more steps into the room. At first he'd thought that the chamber was empty, then he saw that it wasn't. One living and one for the morgue, as GalSec reports would have put it.

If Ruth Gironde had done the job on the hesher Kornelis, she'd done it well. The delicately made-up face was still contorted in the horror of death, several minor cuts marring some of its beauty. It looked as though she'd somehow got hold of a knife and come at him without any warning, slashing and cutting at Kornelis, ripping him apart. Both the hands and arms of the boy were badly mutilated, making it look as though he'd tried to defend himself.

Simon knew well the terror of being attacked by a knife. There was a desperate horror in the way the blood spurted and jetted as you tried to get the weapon away from your attacker. Knowing that time lay with him, and that each cut would weaken you more. Simon had heard others talk about it. Had felt it himself. Seen it in men he'd killed. There was a moment when it seemed the best thing to drop your hands and let the assailant cut you as he wished. Get it over with quickly. Stop the biting, stinging pain, and the blood. Lie down and die. That was the moment when you had to fight all the harder.

It looked as though the hesher had failed to fight on. Seeing the mad determination on Ruth Gironde's face as she wielded the blade. Although he'd obviously been killed in another part of the room and dragged there, the pool of blood leaking round the sagging corpse showed his death had been recent.

Corman hardly looked at it, being more interested in the displays on the screens. Simon was vastly more interested in the man who sat watching the screens in one of the black chairs. Tied with thin, silver wire by the arms and legs. Straining round to look at who'd come in, smiling crookedly when he saw Simon and the gun.

'Sorry I can't stand up and greet you properly. Seem to be a bit tied up with things.'

Simon grinned, despite the gravity of the situation. 'Hello, Bogie. Good to see you.'

If it had just been Razan doing the tying, Simon would definitely have fancied his chances. It was clear that Corman's assessment of the man was right. He was just a functioning doll that walked and talked and did his master's bidding. But it was Corman who was in charge. He did the actual binding himself, but he didn't make the mistake of holding the gun on Simon and then getting caught. He simply told Razan to stand with the thin barrel of the needler pressed to Bogie's neck.

'I hate to have to say this, Simon, my dear young friend, but if you make one false move, then your comrade gets it. If I may be allowed to make a small jest, then I would admit that I have found Bogart something of a pain in the neck. Perhaps it might be possible for me to repay that.'

Bogie laughed at that. Laughed so loudly and so long that the sarcastic noise wiped the self-indulgent smile off Corman's face and made Razan's bony finger whiten on the trigger of the needle-gun.

'I would be happy to have you die now, but there are things that I must do first. Our guests are almost ready for their last rites.'

'Or wrongs,' whispered Bogart, just loud enough for them all to hear.

Face unchanged, Corman waddled over to where Bogart was tied and slapped him as hard as he could across the face, almost knocking him to the floor. His mouth worked, and he was breathing even more heavily when he returned to the task of finishing tying up Rack. Bogie shook his head and spat out a mouthful of blood.

'Bogart, I am not a violent man. Not usually, but your foolish flippancy pushed me too far. I recommend that you do not do that again.' He laughed, his self-assurance nearly re-covered. 'There. Well tied, my dear boy? Excellent. Now I shall leave you to the good offices of Razan here and let you watch the show. Make the most of it, my friends. I fear that there might not be such another.'

With that excellent exit line, Harley Corman strode from the control-room, leaving Razan with his needle-gun, perched on one of the chairs, watching the two bound men.

Most of the screens showed only static views of the junctions of corridors or rooms. The one of the lounge showed Corman as he bustled through on his way to the cryogenic labs. There was also a distant view of space outside the station, and that revealed an interesting sight. Still not much more than a silver speck, the new shuttle was speeding nearer to Paradise. At a guess, Simon reckoned that it would be with them in about two hours. Maybe less.

'Can we talk?' he asked Razan.

The tall man was leaning against one of the further consoles, intently watching the scene in the actual cryogenic lab, where the last survivors of the party were being prepared for their sleep. The Exalted Leader, who was now neither exalted nor a leader, was still shaking from the experience of Kornelis being murdered by the mad Ruth Gironde, Simon's attack on him and then the capture and roping of the two GalSec officers. His empire had fallen about his ears, and he was obviously still not ready to face all the possibilities, nor begin to answer the questions that were on their way.

'What? Talk? I suppose so. Harley Corman didn't say you weren't to, did he? Yes, but talk quietly. I want to hear what's going on in there. I love to hear what they say just before they go on that great ship that carries them over the dark waters of death into the vale of happiness and the land where there is no pain and suffering. Only a great joy and exultation in life!'

Razan's voice had become raised as he talked on, his skull-like face lighting with the fervour of a preacher. Hands quivering, a nervous smile on his lips, he reached over and turned up the volume on one of the speakers.

'You believe totally in what Corman's told you, don't you? About cryogenics?'

'Of course. Now hold your tongues or talk quietly if you wish. I want to listen.'

While he became involved in the activities in the freezing room, which seemed to be mainly the mixing and drinking of various preparations, Bogie whispered to Simon what had happened. The slap from Corman didn't seem to have harmed him, though there was a small cut near his lip and the livid mark of the open hand across his cheek.

It only took a couple of minutes to tell him about the dead sentry and finding Gironde rotting in his disconnected capsule. The mad Ruth Gironde and the capture by Razan and the young boy, Kornelis.

'What'd she kill him with?'

'Knife. There was a surgical scalpel on one of the benches and she went for him with that. He was holding a needler as well, but he never had a chance. She cut his hands badly and he sort of crumpled up. He kept crying for a long time, Simon. Like an animal. Razan wasn't there. She kept hacking away at him, even after he was dead. I can still hear the hiss of the blade and the sucking noise as she drew it through his flesh. Not nice at all.'

'Keep your voices down or I'll have to gag you both. I mean it.'

'What happened after she wasted him?' Simon kept his voice low, leaning as far across towards his partner as the tight wires would allow. All the time, he was keeping one eye on the vid monitor screens, but there was still nothing happening.

'She started to laugh. Sang a little song. Cried a bit. Talked about her lover, who is obviously as good as dead right now. I tried to get her to come and release me, but she regarded me

124

as a threat. When she's totally mad, she doesn't make sense. When she's sane, she realises the full scene, and then she freaks right out back to madness. Most of the time she prefers a sort of half-world between the two, where Wallace is still alive and everything's going to be all right. That's why she's going through with this freezing.'

'That's what she was like,' said Simon, describing quickly what had happened back in the lounge.

'Yeah. She said she'd have to go and say goodbye to everyone otherwise you'd get suspicious. Left the body, dropped the knife and ran out of the door behind us. 'Bout one second later in comes the skeleton over there through the other door. Sees the butchered hesher and drags him to where he is now, crying over him. Gets up, and I think he's going to do for me. Changes his mind and goes running off after Mrs Gironde. That's just about all.'

'Yeah.' Simon looked round the vast room, watching Razan staring intently at the vids, involved in the tiny figures of the guests. Ruth Gironde had joined them, accompanied by Corman, dwarfed by him. He held her arm, and was explaining some story to the others as to why she was late and how the two gallant officers were watching in comfort. Reassuring the nerves that obviously afflicted all of them. Even the imperturbable Strafford.

The rest of the room was huge. Simon tried to do some geometry, working out just how much of the station it actually took up, and coming to the same conclusion he'd reached earlier. There wasn't much room for the frozen bodies of getting on for two hundred rich men and women who'd made the pilgrimage to the golden station of Paradise over the last six months. So where were they? Maybe a smaller station, or had they been secretly taken off? Dangerous, to keep the life-support systems going on a small shuttle. Or, maybe there was another explanation. One that he didn't want to begin to think about. But that fitted a lot of the facts.

'What next, Simon?'

'They freeze. Another shuttle's due soon, so whatever he does has got to be quick. Razan? Razan!!'

'What?' The answer was irritable, the rich tones of the fabulous voice seeming to be fading away under the tension of the moment.

'That shuttle coming. Is there any other ship on the station?'

'No. And shut up about . . . why do you want to know? Think you're going to escape in one?' He laughed at the thought.

'No. I didn't think that *we* were going anywhere. I just wondered if . . . No, it doesn't matter. Silly idea, isn't it? Forget it.'

The hook had gone in. Planted in the mind of the skinny man. He levered himself from his perch and walked quickly over to Simon, the vids temporarily forgotten.

'Rack, what are you getting at? I'm not a fool, you know. Who do you think's going to try and get away? Me? Or Harley Corman?'

Simon shook his head. 'No. Forget it, Razan. Just a silly idea of mine that . . . Never mind. Watch the . . . Aaaaargh!!'

He'd aimed to get Razan's interest, and he'd succeeded rather too well. Leaning over him like the shadow of death itself, his lean fingers had grabbed Rack by the throat, shutting off the air to his lungs and the supply of blood to his brain. He shook his head, but the fingers were like bands of steel. He felt his head swimming and his eyes popping from their sockets.

'Tell me what you mean, Rack! Or I'll break your stinking neck. What do you mean?'

Simon was near the edge. Vaguely, like words drifting through layers of freezing fog, he heard Bogie shouting at Razan. Screaming at him to let go or he'd never find out what they meant. Gradually, slowly, the grip relaxed, and he found that he could breathe again. But his throat was still crushed and sore. Pain that he knew would linger for weeks. If he was allowed to live that long. Somehow, he didn't see Corman leaving them alive.

'Now. I let you live. So tell me what you're trying to say.'

'All right. All right.' He didn't have to fake the distress he was feeling. The soreness was too real. 'It's just that I think that your boss is getting ready to perform one of his famous disappearing acts. He's very well known for them. I guess he's going to skip with the credits and leave you holding an empty bag full of death. Waiting for the next shuttle. He'll be gone.'

'No.' A long pause. 'No. He wouldn't do that. Couldn't anyway. No other ship . . . No, you're trying to trick me, aren't you?'

'You asked me, and I told you. Now let's forget it, shall we? As long as you know everything that goes on in Paradise. Like where the frozen bodies are stored.'

In the stillness, they clearly heard Corman giving his final instructions to the guests. How to lie. How to breathe. They were all listening intently, a small circle about his huge bulk, all in their gowns. Razan said nothing, walking back to where he'd been sitting before.

'You do know?'

'Shut up.'

'Don't you? Nearly two hundred bodies. Must be up here somewhere. Where?'

'I don't know.' The confession seemed to be torn from him against his wishes. 'Corman never told me. And . . .'

'You never thought to ask him.'

'I didn't think.' For a moment, they thought he was going to start weeping, so disconsolate was his voice. 'I just kept the people happy. Acted as a manager. He was always in touch with me through a transceiver. I'm not . . . not really all that good at running things myself or thinking things out without help. Harley helped me. I don't know. Where are they?'

'Abraham.' Simon's voice was reproving. 'How would I

127

know? I'm sure that Corman has some very convincing explanation. I just thought that if you didn't know that, then there may be some other things about Paradise you didn't know. Like, maybe there is another little ship. A one-seater. Tucked away?'

Bogart put in a few words. 'Simon. Can't you see you're confusing poor Abraham. Why don't you leave him alone and let him think about that? Think about what's really going on up here. Maybe he can tell us about a certain little gold capsule that vanished.'

'No. Not that. I'm sure that Harley doesn't know anything about that either. When he heard it had been taken he flew into a terrible rage. I think he was worried that it might make you try and stop Paradise running. And he's totally committed to that. And so am I?'

Gently now. 'We know that you are, Abraham. We all know that. But are you sure that Harley is? Really sure about it?'

The dolls on the vid screens were now vanishing, one by one, walking off to their last five minutes alone. The time for prayer, said the brochure.

'It's prayer time,' said Razan, glancing up at the pictures, turning away from the two bound men. 'That means in just five minutes the first of them goes into the capsules. Then it only takes about three minutes per casket and it's all over. Very quick, you know.'

'Are you sure about Corman, Abraham?' Bogart pressed him, in the nearest he could get to a sympathetic voice.

'I believe in Paradise. I believe in it totally and implicitly. There are so many sad and lonely people. I . . . I don't enjoy being this height, you know. I've always been someone for men to laugh at and women to shrink from. But the medics can't do anything for me. They can add height to dwarfs, and they could lop off a few centimetres by cutting slivers of bone from my thighs and calves. But I'd still be a damned freak!' There was real anguish in Razan's voice.

Out of the corner of his eye, Simon saw the shuttle, gradually growing closer as it sped nearer the station. If only the communications hadn't gone down! Still, if the freezing ceremony went on much longer, they might still buy time.

There was a hissing and bubbling from behind them, as the great open vat at the centre of the chamber began to come to sinister life. He strained round, trying to see what it was, but Razan told him.

'The freezer. Don't know quite what. Harley did tell me, but . . . I sort of let it slip from my mind. If you go up on that catwalk round the top layer of instruments, you can see right down into it. The noise means that the process has started. The liquid's already flowing.'

'Then you'd better be quick, Abraham. You were telling us all about belief.'

'Yes. I do believe. And Harley has promised me that I shall also enjoy the great sleep from which the only awakening is to joy and life. At the end of the first year, I shall be allowed to join the rich and the powerful, and I shall only be revived when there is a way of curing my affliction. Harley has promised me. And it will be free for the services that I have rendered him and Paradise.'

'You do have total trust in the success of the system?'

'I don't understand you, Rack; what do you mean by the system?'

'Cryogenics. You've seen it work?'

'Undoubtedly. Every person frozen has come round with no trouble. You doubt it?'

'Kornelis was a good friend of Corman? And he was the only one ever to be thawed out?'

'Yes, but . . . I don't know. You're trying to trick me! When we first knew that two GalSec officers were coming to Paradise, Harley said that you would be devious and try to catch us out in untruths.'

'Razan, I want you just to take a couple of minutes and think about it. Think whether Corman could just maybe be conning you along. That it just might be some kind of fraud. That there might be a small ship tucked away somewhere on Paradise. Look. They're starting to freeze them now. Watch it and tell us when it's over. It's our necks. But it may just be yours as well. Look. They're beginning!'

They were.

Everything was happening at once. Corman was visible at the edge of one of the screens, smiling unctuously at the guests in their last moments. The shuttle was getting ever closer. Razan was trying to make up his mind, seeking to claw a clear thought from the fog that lay over his brain.

And Simon and Bogie?

They just sat and waited; there really wasn't much else that they could do.

TEN

BETTER THAN NO COMFORT AT ALL

The liquid in the tank bubbled and hissed, a thin stinging mist drifting sluggishly off the top. Razan, ignoring the two officers, paced up and down, now hardly looking at the screens. Twice he stopped in front of Simon, staring at him out of his deep-set, hooded eyes, seeming as though he was about to say something. Then turning away.

Finally, moving slowly, he climbed up the chrome-runged ladder to the balcony that ran right round the central chamber, avoiding the narrow walkway that spidered directly over the huge cauldron of freezing mixture. Veiled in the mist, he leaned against the wall, between two gleaming panels of lights, like a stretched shadow, hands folded in the sleeves of his long gown.

'Simon?' hissed Bogie, trying to watch the Exalted Leader out of the corner of his eye.

'Shut your mouth, Bogart! Or I'll close it permanently for you.'

'Razan. When Corman comes back, why don't you just stay up there out of sight and listen to what he says to us. If we're wrong, then there's no harm done. If we're right, then you can do something about it. You've still got your needler, haven't you?'

'Yes. It's only got three out of its six charges though. I never bothered to keep it loaded fully.'

'So you'll do that?'

'Yes. Yes I will. But I don't believe you about Corman. He's a good man at heart. I knew he's not been good in the past, but he's been good to me, and his work on cryogenics is giving a lot of happiness.'

Simon thought about all the credits it was giving Corman, but decided it was tactful not to mention it to Razan. They were playing a dangerous game with him, particularly as they didn't have any real proof that anything was truly wrong up on Paradise.

'Don't forget, I can hear anything you say, and I'll kill you if you talk to each other. Not another word now until Harley returns. And don't try and warn him that I'm up here. Just say that I've slipped out to my quarters to get ready for the next shuttle.'

That shuttle was still swelling on the vid-screen, now close enough for them to see the occasional puffs of light as the robo-control fired the boosters on minimal course corrections. Simon guessed it would be arriving slightly sooner than Corman had anticipated.

Apart from the noise from the cryogenic vats, the room fell silent. The conversation from the screens had ceased as the last moments of the process neared. Corman had vanished from the vids, but hadn't yet crossed the lounge on his way back. Time drifted slowly by.

Bogie, casually so that Razan wouldn't spot it, began surreptitious finger-talk to Simon. Made more difficult by the tight binding. He asked how they were going to play it when Corman finally came back. Eyes never leaving the vids, Simon gave him the only reply possible. That they would have to wait and play it as it laid. There was nothing else they could do. Unless you're playing the game, you can't bluff, was the old truth. They held no cards, apart from the skinny giant in the shadows above their heads, so all they could do was wait and play it with their wits.

It wouldn't be long now.

Price, looking tiny and frail beside the husky assistants, lay first on the reclining couch, eyes closed, hands folded in front of him. Watching the images on the screens, Simon and Bogie had a re-run of the events they'd first marvelled at only seven days before. The mist started to play around, gradually obscuring the figure, and the sides of the couch rose up to form the protective walls and top of the freezing capsule. The volume was turned down, and they couldn't hear the music chosen by any of their departing comrades.

As soon as Zeta Price had vanished, it was the turn of von Neumann. He stepped quickly to the couch, as though he were hurrying to greet an old friend. Barely a minute elapsed before he too was gone from their sight.

There was still no sign of Corman. Simon guessed that he was still remaining at the controls until it was all over, keeping a final check on the system.

Behind them, they suddenly heard the voice of Abraham Razan, speaking quietly to himself. 'It *does* work. And it's doing so much good to these people. They're all better for their stay with us, and they go to their sleeps cleansed and purged of all their old evil. And when they wake . . .' His voice took on a new note of exultation, much as it had in the past when he'd talked about the great beauty of the process.

Simon looked across at Bogie and shook his head. There wasn't any doubt that Razan was mad.

'The wakening! Oh, the ecstacy of the wakening. Imagine what it must be like. To leave the darkness of a body that has grown stale and old. Diseased or distorted. And to sleep and wake as though only a moment has passed. And to find that you were made new. Healed. Your body was as it had once been. Or as you had always hoped that it would be. You know that I sometimes think that it might be better not to have to wake at all after a sleep at night, knowing what faces one. So many of the lonely who come here. The dying and the afflicted. They clearly wish only for death. Even that would be a relief for most of them. A blessed relief that is denied by society.

But what Harley Corman gives them is so . . . so immeasurably better. So fine. So radiant. So . . .'

'He's coming back. They're freezing the last one now. It's Ruth Gironde.'

While Razan had been talking, both Viki Laurel and Rafael Strafford had lain down and the white mist had played about them and they'd fallen asleep and vanished into the gleaming caskets. Now it was Ruth Gironde. Last survivor of the party.

She was led in by two assistants, seeming as though they were having to hold her upright. The beautiful head drooped and the eyes blinked like someone suddenly encountering a strong light. She lay down, helped by the men, folding her hands as the others had done. Although the picture was soundless, they all saw her lips move just as the gases enveloped her. She whispered the one word 'Krishna' and then disappeared, the sides of the capsule sliding smoothly up to encase her in the cold white fastness.

After that, the vids showed static scenes. The capsules were wheeled away, and the mist cleared from the cryogenics rooms. Still Corman didn't reappear. The far screen showed the shuttle was now very near, beginning its actual landing manoeuvres. Despite the spatial distortion of the vids in deep space, it was obviously now extremely close. Simon flicked a finger at Bogie, telling him to watch it. Asking him how long he thought before it docked. Pursing his lips, Bogie signalled back ten minutes. Which was about what Simon had reckoned.

Razan had fallen silent, retreating into the shadows above the vat. The liquid had ceased to bubble, but a faint mist still rose from it, trickling down the sides of the huge container. Simon's eyes went to the screen showing the main lounge. Ignoring the camera he knew was revealing him, Corman strode quickly across it, on his way back to the control area.

'Remember. One word at all to him, and I'll kill you first.' Razan's voice hissed out at them like the whisper of death from an opened tomb.

They heard Corman's breathing long before he actually appeared in the room, sighing and panting like a warp engine with both compressors failed. It rose even above the clicking of the contacts in the main control board, and the sinister sounds of the freezer vat.

'Well, upon my soul, gentlemen. That was a job well done, though I do say so myself. A group of guests that I never truly expected to be able to see the back of. Where's my dear friend Abraham?'

Simon answered him. 'Razan's gone to his quarters ready for the next shuttle. Said he felt ill for some reason.'

He wanted to give Corman something to take his mind off the imminent arrival of the next load of guests in Paradise. Once he really looked at the end vid he'd see for himself how close that time was.

'Ill? Poor Abraham. I fear he's rarely well. And if he's ill now, then the news he'll soon discover will send him into a positive decline.'

'News?' Bogie twisted round to face the fat man, who stood looking benignly at them, hand holding a needler, absurdly small among the swollen fingers.

To make the talk easier, Corman moved round so that he half-faced them, the shadows of the catwalk just at the edge of his vision. 'There. That's more comfortable. Wouldn't want either of you two dear old companions to suffer from a stiff neck on my behalf.'

'Bogie asked you what news you had for Razan?'

'Yes, Simon. And I heard him ask it. Not just for him. News that has some significance to both of you as well. It concerns my immediate plans for Paradise. I shall be leaving it very shortly, after I have made sure that none of my debts remains unpaid.'

'How? On the shuttle?'

Corman laughed, genuinely amused by the question. 'No. No, indeed. I fear that some of the happenings recently may

135

affect the wishes of the next lot of guests. I have a small ship hidden away near one of the entry ports. My departure will be a sad loss to all, but I have a few necessities of life already packed. A few credits to keep me in the manner to which I hope to become accustomed, and then a few more for my old age.'

'What about Paradise?'

'A reasonable question, but then again you are always a most reasonable person, Simon. Since it will shortly all come out anyway, I might allow myself the small pleasure of telling you about it. It's the least I can do. Paradise, my dear friends, is a trick. A cheat. I have not discovered a freezing process. Or, if I am to be perfectly accurate, I have found a technique that freezes people to such an extent that they die within twelve seconds. Sadly, I have found no way that they can be brought to life again.'

It was shattering. Although Simon had suspected that something wasn't right on Paradise, he'd never guessed that the whole thing was a sham. A massive con-trick. A fraud so insolent and so gigantic that it had never occurred to anyone that it could be false. He shook his head, wondering what sort of effect this must be having on the listening Razan.

'How did you set it up? Must have cost millions in the first place.'

'Indeed it did, Simon. Indeed it did. But you would be surprised how many foolish folk came rushing to me, pressing credits into my hands to help finance me once they'd seen a most elementary magician's trick designed to demonstrate that I had truly mastered the art of cryogenics. That, plus a few special effects and a lot of dressing, created Paradise. Though I do say so, I think that the phrase: "New Life For Old" was quite a helpful inspiration.'

Still nothing from Razan. Simon wondered if he could even hear what was being said above the noise of liquids equalising pressures in the tank. Raising his voice, he asked Corman: 'The bodies. Where are all the bodies you've butchered?'

'Tut, tut. I thought better of you than such a crude expression. "Butchered!" That is unworthy of you, Simon. I merely helped them some of the way towards their goal of a second life. I aided them out of this one. You have seen for yourself how glad most of them were to go. Sadly, I wasn't able to help them *all* of the way. And the remains? Aah. I thought that you might ask that. It was the one great weakness if anyone had become suspicious. Corpses take up space and, as you can see, there is not enough of that precious commodity in the station. No. I personally took charge of that aspect of the operation. The caskets vanished into the vaporiser and are circling somewhere round us, even as I speak. A thin shield of invisible fragments.'

It was a stunningly simple plot. One that could have gone on indefinitely. 'Why six months?'

'Because I couldn't hope to keep it secret for ever and a day. Even a fool like poor dear Abraham would have finally wondered where all the hundreds of caskets were going. And there would be people who would want only to be frozen for a short period. I believe that the lovely Miss Laurel only wished to be processed for six months. That initial period is now up and I am moving on. I have enough credits to last me for several years. I think it unlikely that our paths will cross again, Simon. I greet that thought with a strange mixture of relief and regret.'

Where *was* Razan? He was leaving it damnably late. The shadows on the balcony were deep and hard to penetrate, but Simon thought he detected a flicker of movement up there. Directly above the cauldron.

'So? What happens now, Corman? You know that every detail in GalSec will be after you. Murder on this sort of scale hardly means you'll get overlooked.'

'Murder? Simon, my dear friend. Every person who came up here signed release forms in the unlikely eventuality of anything going wrong. It was like a . . .'

'Licence to kill,' commented Bogie wryly.

'Yes. Yes, I suppose that it might possibly be called that. I like the way you face facts, my dear Bogart. It is one of your more attractive facets. So, you see there is very little murder really. Certainly nothing to call out the militia over.'

'What about Bulman?'

The fat man shook his head so violently, jowls wobbling. 'That is not something to lay at my door, Simon. Though I would hardly blame you if you doubted my word. But a man at the brink of death always tells the truth, they say.'

'You aren't at the brink of death. Are you?' asked Bogie, unable to hide his pleasure at the thought.

'Not me, Bogie. But you both are, and there would be no reason for *me* to lie. I give you my word that it was not done by me or with my knowledge. I suspect it has to have been one of the last set of guests. Strafford would be my guess. Whoever it was had no chance to pass it on, and must have been counting on using it as a passport to wealth on his defrosting.'

Simon laughed. 'That is bloody ironic, Corman. They're all dead, thinking they were going to a second life. Whatever else you've done, you've saved the Federation from a lot of trouble.'

Corman patted him on the shoulder, smiling happily. 'Splendid. You see how fine it is to be a good loser. Indeed, you may lose in our little game, but your mission will be judged a success. The genetic information is safe for all eternity. Nobody has yet returned to life from beyond the grave. Unless you count that prophet from Galilee thousands of years ago. Now, the time has come, unless there are any more questions from either of you . . .'

Stepping back from them, Corman pressed the 'ready' button on the needler. Simon tensed his body, straining every muscle in a last attempt to avoid death. But the wires were too tightly knotted. He could see Bogie in the other chair making a similar effort.

'I'm sorry, my dear boy. Nobody else on the station knows what's happened. The rehabs are too stupid and Razan too innocent. Your superiors will recognise the niceties of the legal position and won't expend man-power to chase me. But the two of you might just hold some kind of grudge and pursue me. A couple of shots will remedy that. Believe me, it has been pleasant knowing you both.'

The barrel of a needle-gun is only a few millimetres in diameter, yet it looked like the main tubes of a star-ship to Simon as Corman pointed it at him. 'The shortest farewells are the best, Simon.'

'That's enough, Corman, you murdering liar!'

The scream was accompanied by the crack of a needler, and the crash as it struck the control panel just beyond Simon's shoulder. Corman jumped, facing the spread of the chamber, looking for his assailant.

A second bolt hissed out from the catwalk, exploding on the plasteel floor with a burst of raw power. Corman skipped surprisingly lightly behind a central control unit, peeking round, risking a couple of shots at the lean shadow above him.

'You can do better than that, Corman.'

The fat man tapped at the floor with his fingers in the vaguely irritated manner of a man whose transport is a couple of minutes late. He looked across at Simon, still tied immovably in his seat, and at Bogie, who was still trying to see where Razan was.

'I have to thank you for this, Simon. My dear boy, I must learn to avoid this silly error of underestimating your capacity for interference. Abraham would never have thought of this himself. Dear, dear. And I helped you by being so foolish and boastful. Pride cometh before a fall, as they say. But I imagine it will only take me a couple of minutes to rid myself of that annoyance, and then I shall return for you.'

Another quick shot up into the dimness, and then Corman moved, waddling like some bloated spider across the floor, until he was pressed against the side of the central vat of liquid. Dampness frosted its side, trickling down the smooth metal.

'Abraham! Come down and I'll take you with me. This shooting is foolishness.'

There was no answer. With a chill, Simon realised that the Exalted Leader must only have one shot left in his six-shot needler. Corman had three.

'Two hundred deaths,' shouted Razan, his voice on the outer edge of madness. 'Two hundred! ! !'

As he shouted, he made his move. But his height was against him, making it hard for him to move fast. He came out of the darkness, gun in hand, seeming even taller by the distance he was above them. Face white as a bone, eyes glowing silver, he looked like some dreadful avenging angel. He fired once, the bolt splashing harmlessly on the floor, sending a thread of liquid fire that died as soon as it was born.

Corman fired twice, and again, two of the shots striking home. With a cry of agony and despair, the tall man was sent flying, flames blossoming on the back and hem of his cloak, to fall across the framework of tubing that latticed over the top of the tank of freezing liquid. With a gigantic effort, Razan just managed to hang on one of the bars, legs dangling towards the tank. Unable to get up, and knowing it meant death to let go.

'Corman. Help me up. Help me up, or shoot me again! Not a death like this, Corman. I beg you.'

The fat man stood up cautiously, watching the hanging body of his lieutenant, his needler still trained on it. Simon and Bogie also watched the tableau. He turned to look at them, breathing hard. 'So. Two hundred and one. Poor Abraham. I don't think I have the time to spare to put him out of his misery.'

'I'm slipping. Please! !'

The smoke from the smouldering robes hung in the still air.

From where they sat, Simon and Bogie could only see one hand, gripping the metal framework, fingers white with the strain. No man could hang like that for long.

'Kill him, Corman. At least do him that favour.'

'Very well, my friend. Him first, and then . . .' he aimed quickly and squeezed the trigger of the needler. There was only the hollow whine of an empty charge. He didn't waste any time on futile anger. Merely turned round and pointed it at Simon, depressing the firing button once more. The same thing happened.

Rack had been counting the shots, as he always did, and had known that the needler was empty. But it was never a pleasant experience, facing a gun.

'So. I have an extra charge in my . . .'

The scene was interrupted by a klaxon horn and a loud recorded voice over the speakers. 'Attention all Paradise personnel! The shuttle is now docking! Attention all Paradise personnel. The shuttle is now docking!'

Corman closed his eyes, obviously weighing up what he wanted to do against the risk. The risk won, as Simon had hoped it might.

'I must be away. I'm sorry, Abraham. I can do nothing for you. Simon. Bogart. Fate being what it is, I can always suppose we might meet again. As I said before, the shortest farewells are the best.' Corman moved quickly to the door that led to where his ship was hidden. He turned at the last, and looked back at them. 'In some ways, I do not regret the way luck has played her hand. Goodbye.'

As he went, he winked.

For a moment, there was no sound in the large room. Then, high over their heads, Razan spoke to them. His voice was soft, drained by pain into a shadow of its former glory. 'I am going. My arm. The bolt is working. Thank you for . . . for . . .'

'Try and hang on, Razan. Help'll be here soon.'

'Simon . . . I do not think I want such help . . . not now . . .

Listen . . . while he talked . . . his ship . . . drained fuel and . . . blocked warp valves . . . won't get . . . get far . . . I wanted his new life so much . . . so . . '

It happened so fast and so quietly that neither Simon nor Bogie actually saw it. The weight of his body grew too much for his hand, and there was no longer a will to force it on. There was a faint splash, then a moment or two of bubbling and a burst of mist and fumes from the top of the vat. After that, it was very still.

Neither of them spoke for a moment, sitting bound in their seats, waiting for the inevitable rescue when the staff realised that their masters were gone.

'What'll you tell them? The new guests? They'll be here expecting new life for old and a second chance and all that.'

'The truth, Bogie. That the freezing was all a massive trick, and that everyone concerned has either gone or will soon be gone. That's if Razan did what he said to Corman's ship. He won't go far with damaged warp valves. Just tell them it's all off. No freezing. Not ever.'

'Sort of an offer of cold comfort,' said Bogie, grinning at the relief from tension.

Simon nodded. 'You know, in a way he did offer them a kind of new life, since most of them were sick of their old ones. Yet, it wasn't *truly* a new life.'

'What was it, then?'

'More like the same old death, Bogie. Same old death.'

A Selection of Science Fiction Titles from Sphere

All Sphere Books are available at your bookshop or newsagent, or can be ordered from the following address:

Sphere Books, Cash Sales Department,
P.O. Box 11, Falmouth, Cornwall.

Please send cheque or postal order (no currency), and allow 15p for the first book plus 5p per copy for each additional book ordered up to a maximum of 50p in U.K. or Eire. Overseas customers and B.F.P.O. please allow 20p for the first book and 10p per copy for each additional book.